PERFECTION

KITTY THOMAS

BURLESQUE PRESS

Printed in the United States of America

ISBN-13: 978-1-938639-55-5

Published by Burlesque Press

contact: burlesquepress@nym.hush.com

PUBLISHER'S NOTE:

To Darlene G. Thanks for the meme!

And for Annabel Joseph: from one ballet kink lover to another.

1

Today is the happiest day of my life. For a short time, I defined the happiest day of my life as the day I married the perfect man, the wealthy and beautiful Conall Walsh. In the months that followed, I learned just how imperfect he was, until today, three years later, when I'd had enough of this *perfection*.

I just killed him. The body lies at my feet, more blood and gore than I'd expected to be honest. I'm not sure what I thought cutting up a body entailed, but I had to get rid of it. Obviously, I know there is the tub-of-acid option. And I considered that. I really did. But all I could think was wouldn't it be fucked up if I ended up burning my own skin away while trying to destroy the body?

I don't think I processed the idea that I could also have a chainsaw accident. And by the time I had that harrowing thought, he was already in nineteen pieces while I contemplated if I needed to make his torso any smaller or was this enough? Now the possibility that I could injure myself with the chainsaw has squirreled its way into my brain. No, we're done here. Nineteen pieces. It'll have to do.

I put what's left of the perfect man into several black heavy duty garbage bags. I take down all the plastic wrap I'd taped up and laid down to catch everything. I've seen enough TV to know how this is done. Except on TV you don't really see everything about clean-up, do you? If I had, blood wouldn't have slipped out of the plastic onto the white tile floor of the master bathroom.

Fuck me. That is never coming out of the grout.

I take him out to the ocean... in his own boat. He named that boat after some side piece he was fucking. Probably fucked her yesterday. There's something really satisfying about taking him on his last ride on the boat he used to rub Stella Crenshaw in my face. *The Delectable Stella* it's called. That fake-titted bimbo he was fucking in his office. I imagine him bending her over the copy machine after office hours, her fake nails digging into the hard plastic of the machine while she fakes her orgasm. Because there is no way she wasn't faking it. Part of that is because Conall is bad in bed, and the other part is... well, everything else about her is fake. What's one more thing?

My husband was a real piece of work, and if fucking his secretary had been the worst thing he'd done to me, we'd just be looking at a divorce. I asked for a divorce; he told me if I left him, he'd kill me. I don't know why. After all, he had The Delectable Stella. But some men just need a Delectable Stella and a Punching Bag Cassia.

I'm not sure how far out to take him. You never see that part on TV. You just see the murder, then suddenly there's a boat out on the ocean, and the bags are going into the water in the dead of night. I wonder suddenly if beachfront property is so expensive because of the ease of body disposal. That's a perk you can't get in the heartland.

I finally decide I'm probably out far enough and dump the bags over the edge. I remembered to weigh them down with heavy rocks. Otherwise, the bags will float to the top, some deep sea fisherman will pull it in with his haul, and then the investigation starts.

It's three a.m. when I finally get back home. The house is so quiet. No yelling. No glass crashing against the wall. No screams (mine). No sound of my body being slammed against the wall. I really don't know how I've survived this long. I guess a dancer's body is built for a certain amount of abuse. But not this much. And not this kind. One of our more recent fights pops into my mind.

"Are you fucking him?"

"Who?"

"You know who."

"He's my dance partner. And he has a boyfriend. I didn't date other dancers in the company even before we met. You know that."

I spend another half hour standing in the bathroom staring at the bloodstains in the grout. Am I in shock? Am I a sociopath? Why don't I feel anything? I just feel... numb. Relieved and numb. But I don't feel free. What if I get caught? What if I go to prison for this? I couldn't live another day with him, and there was no other way out. He closed off all my other options.

A jury wouldn't care about that.

What is wrong with me? I still can't believe I was able to just cut up a body like that... the body of a man I once thought I loved. I think it was the adrenaline. The poison worked fast, and then there was no backing out. I just had to get rid of the body. I couldn't think about it. I just did it.

And now I can't stop staring at the grout—the last evidence of the man who sold me all the lies of a perfect life. He'd come in and rescued me out of poverty. He'd given me everything—or at least that's how it looked to everyone else.

Professional dance pays shit, especially when you aren't a principal. You have to work your way up through the hierarchy, and a lot of dancers never get out of the *corps de ballet*. And in truth, the dance world is SO competitive that being in the corps of a decent company is still the dream and much more than many can ever hope for. So I don't complain. I'm lucky.

I sometimes get a small solo, and I often have a *pas de deux* partner in some of the group scenes who lets me pretend for a moment out on that stage that I have some greater role, some greater career and that those screaming cheers from the audience at the end of everything are for me and me alone. I just want someone to really see me.

But I'm background. Nobody notices me. They don't know my name. I'm there to make the principals look more epic because of all the background dancers swirling around them in perfect time. I'm lucky I get to do what I love, even if I'll never be known for it or ever make any real money at it. In a way, Conall was my patron. He funded my ability to keep dancing without worrying how I would also keep eating.

I'm supposed to be in the studio for rehearsal at eight in the morning. We're opening with Swan Lake in the repertoire this season. I'll probably be dancing the same part in the corps that I always dance. I know this part. I've known it for ages, but we still have to rehearse. I have to get my shit together, get a few hours' sleep, and dance like I didn't just kill a man.

❄

WHEN I STEP INTO THE STUDIO, EVERYTHING SEEMS SURREAL, OR hyper-real, or... something. Every sound is harsh and loud. Every color too bright. Every smell an assault. It's like a hangover, except I wasn't drinking last night. Maybe it's a murder hangover. Is that a thing? How would I know? It's not like I do this every week.

The hyper-reality of life around me stands in stark contrast to the unreality of my own sense of self. I feel like I'm glitching in and out of existence, accompanied by a static electric hum. I look up to find a fluorescent light in the studio hallway flickering in and out and roll my eyes at myself. *Get a grip, Cassia.*

"We're in studio B today," Melinda says to me as she passes.

"Thanks," I murmur, not meeting her eyes.

My partner walks up then. "Oh honey, you look like shit. Do I need to kill that motherfucker?"

I let out a too-loud hysterical laugh. In the first place, Henry is far more Fashion Week Aficionado than Aspiring Killer. He knows Conall hurts me. Or... hurt me. He's been trying to get me to leave him for more months than I can count. I didn't tell him about the death threats. I didn't tell the police about them, either, because it wouldn't matter. Conall Walsh is untouchable in this city. He'd hire someone to end me and make it look like an accident.

Or maybe worse... he would have ripped away my financial safety net, and I might have had to quit dancing. A lot of the company people group up for living expenses, but I'm not factored into their plans. I'm married to a man with money. In their minds, I don't need them. And nobody has any room right now in their apartments anyway.

"He went out of town. I just didn't get much sleep last night," I say.

It's not a complete lie. Conall was *supposed* to go out of

town. That's why I chose last night. And technically, he is out of town. We were definitely outside the city limits when I dumped the body in the ocean.

Most people won't miss him for a while. Besides, I'm sure he didn't have business. His business was a swank luxury vacation with Delectable Stella. She works hard leaning over that copier, letting him finger her under her skirt after all.

"Good," Henry says. "Not about the sleep. Good that he's out of town. We should have a movie night while he's gone."

"Sure," I say, wondering if I can ever let Henry inside my house again with the pink stains in the bathroom grout.

"Oh, by the way, Happy Birthday!" He pulls me into a tight hug. "I am definitely taking you out tonight!"

Oh, yeah. That was today. Twenty-four. It feels like a clock on my life. Twenty-four hours in a day. Twenty-four years before your chances of becoming a principal start to slip into the background forever. Ballet is the only profession where twenty-four starts to feel like you should be putting in a good word for yourself at all the better nursing homes.

I've been with the company for three years now; three or four years is pretty standard here to get raised out of the corps, but I know the sands of time are draining away on my dream. And as much as I try to put on a brave face and be gracious and acknowledge the luck of being able to do what I love, deep down I know I'll never be the swan queen or Giselle or Juliet or the Firebird. I'll always be scenery.

Even so, I love being on that stage, the way I move through the air, floating, flying. Henry's hands on my waist, lifting me up, spinning me around like we're at some old-fashioned fancy party, except that I'm in *pointe* shoes.

The corps drifts into Studio B for warmups. I stop by a set of lockers to put my extraneous things away. There is a bright red balloon attached to my locker, with "Happy Birthday" splashed in metallic gold lettering on the front. At least it isn't *pointe* shoes. Not that I don't love *pointe* shoes—at the same time I hate them—but on balloons they seem to be geared to pre-teen girls. And that would only make me feel old.

I open my locker to find a gold glittery envelope with my name on it. I smile, wondering if it's from Henry or Melinda. Maybe it's even from the ballet master. Maybe it's an invitation to audition for a larger role.

Yes, I still have ridiculous fantasies like that—even after three years here. Inside is a very elegant birthday card with a ballerina on it. But this ballerina is adult and sophisticated, far removed from the pink canopy beds and soft ballet shoes of girlhood.

Inside the card with its pre-packaged well-wishes, is another card. It's a stiff white note card. Expensive card stock. And my heart leaps in my throat for a moment wondering if it IS an invitation to audition. But those are not the words typed onto the card.

You were a very bad girl. If you don't want me to report what I know about last night, meet me at the old opera house after rehearsal. I will tell you the price of my silence when you arrive. If you speak of this or bring anyone with you... no deal.

I quickly stuff the note back into the card and shove it into my locker. I look around the hallway but everyone is already in the rehearsal room warming up. When I enter Studio B, the door clangs behind me. Everyone looks up from the barre.

But I'm still ten minutes early, not ideal for getting shoes on and warm-up time, but I'm not late. The ballet master looks up from his notes, smiles at me, and nods to indicate an empty spot at the barre. I smile back. He goes back to his notes. He normally comes in right at class time, so it's jarring to see him now as though I'm late and doing something wrong by coming into the studio.

He's got this really long Russian name that starts with a V that nobody can pronounce. So we were all instructed to call him Mr. V. He's in his early fifties and danced with the Bolshoi. I drop my bag as quietly as possible in one of the corners, take off my outer layer of clothes, and put on my soft ballet shoes and leg warmers.

I'm grateful we aren't starting with *pointe* work today because those shoes take longer to get on than simple ballet shoes. I move to the indicated empty spot at the barre and start warming up. Some *pliés*, *tendus*, several *ronds de jambe* because my hips tend to get tight. I do a few small jumps and then some stretches on the floor. I have just enough time to get through my most basic warm-up routine when Mr. V clears his throat. Everyone stops what they're doing and stands, facing him.

There is something sort of militaristic about ballet. On the stage it's all about flow and grace, but there is discipline and precision beneath this illusion. Life in a classical ballet company is pretty regimented. Some people would hate this life, but I love it. I love knowing exactly what I'm supposed to be doing. I love that I don't have to make the decisions. I just have to execute the movement as perfectly as possible.

"We'll be starting the season with Swan Lake. Casting was posted just this morning, so if you haven't seen it yet, be sure to check the list," Mr. V says.

I haven't seen the casting list yet, but as a member of the corps, it's probably not anything spectacular. I might be lucky and get a solo, but ultimately, what does it matter which nameless character I play?

2

The next two hours go by in a blur. It's kind of hard to focus and be present in the moment when you have a blackmailer threatening to expose your crimes to the authorities. Even so, somehow I didn't fuck up too badly in class. Poor Melinda kept falling out of her turns, and everyone else's minor ballet misdemeanors were ignored as she received the full weight of Mr. V.'s unhappy attention.

"Dinner and drinks on me, birthday girl," Henry says, attaching himself to me like an octopus as we exit Studio B. I want to laugh at his antics, but I can't. I have to go to the old opera house. *Tell no one. Bring no one.* What if it's a friend of Conall's who wants personal revenge? The possibility sends a chill down my spine.

"I can't. I have somewhere I have to be tonight, but we can do it tomorrow. I promise."

Henry looks suspicious. "Girl, if you think I'm going to let you snuggle in bed and binge-watch TV and cry into a rice cake about your aging grizzled self, you are out of your mind.

It's your birthday, and we're going to celebrate, because I, for one, am glad you've made it another year."

"I'm so tired. I got no sleep last night. I have to rest. Please. I need to come to terms with twenty-four and regroup. Tomorrow, I swear," I plead. This is actually a convincing lie. The angst of twenty-four cannot be overstated.

He sighs. "Okay, fine. But we *will* celebrate, so prepare yourself."

I force a laugh at that.

I know the only reason he's letting this go is because I look like shit. Murder and insomnia will do that to a girl. He hugs me again.

"But don't binge-watch. Sleep. Promise me. And use that milk and honey mask I gave you. You need it. Don't get me started on those circles under your eyes."

"Yes, Mother. I promise." I wish I could tell Henry. I wish I could tell anyone about the expensive white card nestled inside the birthday wishes in the glittery gold envelope.

The old opera house is a historic landmark. I don't think it's actually officially on the registry of protected historic buildings, but nobody wants to tear it down. At the same time, the city doesn't have the money to restore it, and no wealthy benefactors have come forward to fund such an ambitious project.

So it sits in limbo—a ghost clinging to this world—and no one else can let it go, either. Neither living nor dead, the building stands enormous, imposing, creepy as fuck. There is no good to be had in this building. It's probably not even unlocked.

I try one of the elegant front doors. Yep. Locked. But then I realize there's a small rolled-up paper slipped under the handle. I pull it out.

The side door, Ms. Lane.

What an asshole. Somehow this note makes me think whoever is in the building isn't going to kill me. I don't know why I think that, but this little bit of sarcasm makes me irrationally think that at least my life is safe. I can feel the eye roll in the note. It's exasperation—like this person knew I'd try the front door, which of course wouldn't be unlocked. But why would any door be unlocked? Whoever this is obviously has a key.

As I walk around to the side entrance, I try to think of who could know my secret. Did they see me at the house? Or at the boat? Or both? Did they follow me? Do I have a stalker? Again, is it a friend of Conall's? It's not like people don't know I dance at the company. It wouldn't be hard for anyone to slip in and drop a card into my locker—and not unusual, either, with it being my birthday.

I open the side door and step into the lobby. There's a light coming from the concession stand, illuminating everything in a sort of creepy glow. Why is there electricity on? Surely the city would have shut it off. There was a rumor someone bought the place about a year ago. Still, it was just a rumor, and when nothing came of it, no renovations, no announcements, we all just went back to our lives.

There are a few popcorn boxes littering the floor and an old empty cup that once held some soft drink or other. There's a thick layer of dust on everything. It looks like a zombie apocalypse swept through. I find the popcorn boxes strange. Is there some precognition about places shutting down? Does the cleaning staff just say 'fuck it' after that final night? Is there so little pride in the place that you can't at least make the effort to leave it nice even if you know no one else will ever see it again?

Then I realize the light is on at the concession area

because there's a sign propped up on the counter, and I'm meant to be able to read it.

Go to the stage, Ms. Lane.

I'm so tempted to run out of the building, get in my car, and just drive. Leave town. But then I get a hold on myself and take a deep breath. This person wants money. That's what blackmail is. Just give them the money and go on with life.

But the creepiness of this place has to be experienced to be appreciated. I keep looking over my shoulder every second, fearing my blackmailer will jump out and pounce on me. I'm the idiot girl in the horror movie doing all the stupid shit that leads to her grisly murder in the second act. But I don't have a lot of options here.

I can't go to the police because then they'll want to know what this person knows. Goodbye dance career, hello prison. What other choice do I have but to do what this person wants? And just hope it's an amount of money I have access to or that a payment plan is acceptable.

Conall didn't exactly give me *carte blanche* on the money. I'm not even sure yet how I'll handle that. He gave me a small allowance in a separate account, and everything else he kept blocked and private. A sudden panic seizes me as I worry Conall's money won't continue to support me. If he's missing, it will be a long time before he's legally declared dead. I might not have access to most of the money for a very long time.

I mean, the house is paid for, and the bills are on auto-pay. And I do get paid something as a dancer. Of course it's enough. I won't starve. I have a roof. I have clothes and everything I need. But it isn't enough to pay a blackmailer, not even a pittance. I swallow hard and fight back the tears at that thought.

I pass underneath a grand staircase that curves around on both sides. At the top is the second level balcony seating. I go through the middle set of double doors on the main floor. There is a spotlight on the stage, and a single practice ballet barre. A long rectangular table is upstage, stage left next to the wings. And there's a chair pushed neatly under the table. Small theater guide lights in the floor illuminate just enough so I can see where I'm walking.

My heart is thundering in my chest. As much as I've tried to convince myself this person just wants money and I'll survive this night, I'm so scared right now I can't think. Somehow it propels me forward faster, like I just can't stand the anticipation of it all.

Whatever is going to happen here, I want to get it over with. I climb the steps onto the stage and stand in the middle, looking wildly around me... into the wings backstage, out into the audience... the balcony... the once-elegant private box seats.

A black vinyl dance tarp is taped to the stage floor. It's brand new. There are no shoe marks or indications that a single living soul has danced across it. This is recent. This was for today. I'm so confused. Why? Why has the stage been transformed into a dance floor? This has to be someone from the company. A principal? The ballet master? But how would they have seen me? Maybe it's a patron of the company. Could I have a stalker who stumbled upon my crime?

I was careful, but I didn't expect to be watched. I didn't expect that there might already be longstanding eyes on me— which is admittedly weird for a professional dancer, practically living onstage.

"Hello? Look, I can get you money. Hello?" I don't mention the limits of my ability to get money right now. I need to just find out my blackmailer's terms. Don't give them a reason to call the police.

There's a crackling sound and then a booming male voice magnified over a speaker.

"I neither need nor want your money, Ms. Lane" It's a smooth, rich baritone. But I can't tell if the voice belongs to someone old or young. And I don't recognize it.

"Do you know he beat me? He threatened to kill me. What was I supposed to do? He practically owned this city. Do you know how much power he had? What other choice did I have?" I shout into the mostly empty theater.

"Do you know how much power *I* have?" he counters.

Obviously a lot if he can get into this building and have electricity running in it. "I don't deserve prison," I say.

"Murder is a serious crime." His tone is similar to the one you'd hear in the principal's office after being caught vandalizing a dumpster behind the school.

"Please..." I feel the hysteria bubbling over as my gaze continues to dart around the cavernous theater, trying to find where he's hiding, what perch he observes me from. "Please..." I say again... "You said you'd tell me your price. How much? Please. I'll pay you anything."

"No, Ms. Lane. Not money. I have plenty of that. The price of my silence is your obedience."

The stillness that follows this announcement is so complete you could hear a pin drop on the black dance tarp. What the hell does that mean?

"Empty out your dance bag in the center of the stage and spread out all the contents," he says.

I freeze at that. There's a gun in my dance bag. I'm not *that* stupid, that I'd just go meet some mysterious blackmailer without going home to get a weapon first. I mean, come on.

"I want to remind you that we aren't in a 1940's noir film. I have a phone on me at all times, and I will use it to report you if you hesitate again."

I take a deep breath. My hands are visibly shaking as I empty out the dance bag, arranging the contents, carefully concealing the gun in a dance sweater.

"What are you hiding from me?" the voice asks again.

I look around the otherwise empty theater, trying desperately to find the source of that voice.

"N-nothing!"

"Do you want to go to prison, Cassia?"

His use of my first name startles me. It feels too familiar in spite of everything.

The voice continues. "No. Lies. I want to see what you're hiding."

I don't know how I thought I would get away with this. Did I think he'd just show up and confront me in some straight forward face-to-face way? Did I think he'd let me see him? Did I think I'd have a clear shot, and he'd just stand politely still while I put a bullet in him?

What the hell was I thinking?

"Last chance to save yourself," he says, his patience running out.

I feel like I'll hyperventilate as I unwrap the gun from the sweater and lay it out on the brightly lit stage. I flinch and look around me as if he'll somehow swoop down, materialize on top of me, and rip me apart for daring to try to defend myself.

He chuckles. "Were you planning to build a body count? Gotten a taste for it, have you?"

"N-no," I stammer.

"No, Sir," he corrects. "I expect a basic level of formality and etiquette when we're in this space together."

Everything inside me freezes at this. *When we're in this space together.*

But I just parrot back, "No, Sir," as I try to wrap my head around what is happening here.

"Good. Now put the gun on the table. You'll be leaving it behind when you go home tonight."

A long breath flows out of me. I'm going home tonight. He's not going to kill me. Then I mentally chastise myself for that thought. He could be lying. He could be in the wings. He could snatch that gun and shoot me with it.

"I-I can't leave the gun," I say.

"Oh? Why is that?"

"It's Conall's gun, he'll..." I was about to say he'll be angry. He'll hit me. I'm so scared I'm not thinking clearly.

"He'll what, Ms. Lane? He'll rise out of the ocean, reassemble, and come after you? Maybe he *does* have more power than me."

"I just... I'm scared. I forgot..."

"You forgot you killed a man, chopped him up, and dumped him in the ocean?"

"I..." He's right. That sounds stupid. But it was only last night. Maybe I am in some kind of shock. The sense of unreality that my day started out in has only gotten worse as the day has progressed. And I'm so tired right now. Some part of me thinks maybe this is a dream. None of this is real. It can't be real.

I can't even remember cutting him up. I can't remember going out in the boat. I remember pieces of it. Showering the blood off. Gathering rocks. Dumping the bags into the water. But there are gaps. Big fucking gaps. Kind of like a dream. What is wrong with me? Is this normal? It's not like there's some killer's anonymous support group I can call to find out what's normal in these situations.

"Now, put the gun on the table and no more weapons. Is that clear?"

"Yes, Sir."

"Good." I can hear the satisfied smile in his voice at my easy expression of formality and etiquette.

I struggle to my feet and try unsuccessfully to stop the tremors moving through me as I pick up the gun, cross the stage, and place it on the table. I sort of hover there, afraid to move away, afraid he'll jump out of the shadows and grab the gun.

"Go back to where you were and sit down. If I wanted you dead, you would be dead. I don't need you to supply me with a weapon."

He's right of course. Everything but the stage is dark. We're isolated in an abandoned building. He knows the layout of this place. I don't know where he is. He's no doubt much stronger than me physically. A gun really is overkill; pardon the pun.

I'm sure this man is with the company. I may not recognize his voice, but he is part of the ballet world. I know he set up this floor and this barre. It wasn't just something left behind. Our company is very strict and formal. No instructor or ballet master is ever referred to by their first name. It's Mr. or Ms. Last Name.

In certain circumstances, it's Sir or Ma'am. Though silence is the rule of the ballet class. There's very little reason to speak. You're told to do something at the barre or in the center, alone or with a partner, and you simply do it. If you make a mistake, you are corrected. And sometimes, if you're lucky, you're allowed to do it again and fix your mistake in that moment rather than have to remember it for the next time.

Obviously, this man isn't going to tell me his name, so of course he will demand to be called Sir.

The disembodied voice fills the theater when he speaks again. He could be anywhere, but he's obviously close enough to have been able to see everything in my bag clearly—though he could have opera glasses to see the details on stage that his seat won't allow.

"Performances are Thursday night through Sunday night. Monday and Tuesday you have all day rehearsals. Wednesday you have off, and you return early Thursday afternoon to prepare for the night's performance."

I know my schedule. But he wants me to know that he knows it, too. Just more evidence he's from the company.

"Therefore," he continues... "you belong to me every Wednesday night from nine p.m. until midnight."

"I... *what*?"

"That is my price, Ms. Lane. You will come here every Wednesday night, and you will obey me."

"I..."

"Pick up the notebook and pen."

There's a dance notebook in the array of contents on the floor. I sit down like he'd previously asked me to and open the notebook to a fresh page. I keep choreography notes and corrections in there. A lot of dancers have these. It's what you do as a professional. I also write down schedules and other various company notes that might slip through the cracks of my mind.

"Make a note. When you arrive each Wednesday night, I want you clean and ready to work. I want you in either a medium gray or plum-colored leotard with a low open-scooped back..."

This is the point where if not for my ballet training, I would interrupt and say I don't have leotards in those two colors, to which he would no doubt tell me to get them. But I don't interrupt him because it just isn't done in my world. When the ballet master speaks, you simply listen. You never interrupt. And somehow my brain has clicked over into dance mode, and I can't bring myself to interrupt his list of orders.

He continues. "Pink tights, pink leg warmers. You may wear black hip warmers if you need them, but no ballet skirts. I want your hair up as you would wear it for class. No makeup. No jewelry. Bring both *pointe* shoes and ballet shoes. Canvas, not leather. And not dirty. Canvas shoes can be washed, and I fucking loathe when dancers don't take advantage of that fact."

He stops. I wait. Finally he says, "Behind you on the barre is a blindfold. I want you to pick it up, go sit at the table, and put it on."

There is, in fact, a black strip of cloth hanging off the edge of the barre. I hadn't noticed it when I first stepped onto the stage. I was too hyper-aware of all the spaces he could be hiding. Finally, all my etiquette training fails me.

"Please..." I say. "Please just let me go."

"You can go if you like. Expect the police at your door in less than an hour."

The tears slide down my cheeks.

"Shhh, Cassia, I'm not going to hurt you. I realize that's impossible to believe right now, but you don't have a lot of choices, so I suggest you take the risk."

I push myself up off the floor and go to the barre. I don't want to go to prison. I want to dance. And this man could make all those dance dreams just stop... forever. There are a lot of other things he could do if I put on that blindfold, but he could do them anyway for all the reasons I've already acknowledged.

My only chance to have a life still worth living tomorrow is to do what he says. I take the scrap of soft black cloth and go sit down at the table. I put the blindfold on.

"Good. Now, place your hands on the table, palms down. And wait."

I wait. Forever. Fall turns to winter and then spring in the space of this eternity. But then I sense him in my space. I feel the brush of air beside me, hear soft footsteps, and I long for the return of that eternity wrapped up in the brief few minutes I waited.

I want to run. I want to rip the blindfold off. But I'm afraid if I see his face, he'll pick up that gun—the weapon I stupidly hand-delivered to him—and just kill me.

Something heavy is placed on the table. Metal or glass, I can't be sure. But then I smell it. Food. Steam is rising up off the dish, wafting to my nose. Then something else, a lighter sound, then something like a glass. A cork pops. Liquid is poured into the glass.

"I'm sorry you missed your birthday dinner. Let me make it up to you. I made lasagna."

I freeze. The tears start to flow down my cheeks again. "Please... don't..."

"Don't what? Don't feed you? You have to eat. And you haven't had dinner."

He sounds so reasonable as he says this. As if any of this were reasonable. But I can't stop the tears. They only come harder. Lasagna is what I made last night for Conall. It's the food I poisoned. Why would he give me lasagna? Is he poisoning me? Maybe he's just a psychopath who wanted to toy with me for a little while and then kill me.

"This is a pretty strong reaction to lasagna," he says mildly. "Why? Is it because that was Conall's final meal? So, what? You're just never going to eat this food again? I make a great lasagna. You can't take this from me."

"Is it going to kill me?"

He chuckles at that. "I told you, I'm not going to kill you. If I wanted to kill you, I wouldn't use a gun, and I wouldn't use poison."

His hands slide around my throat, and I tense. My palms are still flat on the table. I don't bother to claw at him because he doesn't squeeze. It's an object lesson. This is how he would do it... to answer my curiosity, to make me stop spinning the thousand ways I could die at his hands. This is the way he would do it. He would just wrap his hands around my throat... and squeeze. It would take almost no effort on his part.

The amount of power he has to hurt me in this moment nearly levels me. I'm about to have a full-on panic attack. But before I can reach that moment of sheer hysteria, he removes his hands from around my neck. Then he says, "Open," and a steaming bite of lasagna is prodding at my mouth.

I'm still afraid it's poisoned. I can't help it. I don't know this person. And anyone who would do what he's doing... this sick, twisted blackmail... this desire to own my life like this... is not someone I can trust. But I have no choice. I open my mouth and hope it's not poisoned.

This is the best food I've ever had in my mouth. Holy fuck. This man could be a chef. It wasn't an empty boast; he really does make a great lasagna. For a moment I forget to be afraid it's poisoned. It's just that amazing. After a few bites, a glass prods at my lips, and I sip the red wine he offers.

When the food is gone, I hear dishes being removed and then there is another small plate in front of me. I know it's small because of the lighter sound it makes when it settles in front of me. And another glass. Another liquid. This time the liquid comes out of something with a cap you screw off. I can hear it. My hearing is so acute in this moment, listening for every single tiny clue for what's coming next, even as I'm terrified to know.

I flinch when I hear and smell a match being lit.

"Relax," he whispers in my ear.

As if that's even a possibility. Having a psycho light a match near you while you're blindfolded isn't exactly something that inspires relaxation in most normal people.

"It's your birthday candle," he says. "Now, I'm going to remove the blindfold for a moment so you can see your cupcake. If you turn around to look at me, you will be punished."

Punished. I don't know what that means, but I don't want to know.

"Will you turn around and try to look at me?" he asks.

"No, Sir. I don't want to die."

"I didn't say I'd kill you. I said I'd punish you. Or maybe report you. I know you just murdered someone last night, but this obsession with killing is just unhealthy, Ms. Lane."

There's suddenly a flash of knowledge that pops into my head—like that creepy unexplainable psychic intuition people sometimes get. And maybe I'm wrong about this, but I have the sudden very strong feeling that he's already taken a precaution. Maybe he has a ski mask with the mouth cut out to allow unobstructed speech.

I just don't believe he would take this risk with me. He wants to know if I'll turn around and try to find out who he is. If I do that, and he's wearing a mask, I won't have any greater knowledge, and there will be another price to pay for the disobedience.

He removes the blindfold, and I use every ounce of discipline my training has afforded me and resist the urge to turn around. I look straight ahead at a chocolate cupcake, with light pink frosting and a small red candle on top.

He leans close to my ear. "Close your eyes, make a wish, and blow out the candle. But don't tell me what it is, or it won't come true."

What the fuck is happening right now?

I should wish that this man didn't know my secret. I should wish to be free of whatever demands he may make of me. But I can't waste my wish on that. I wish for what I always wish— every year since my fourteenth birthday. I wish to be a principal. I wish to be the star.

I know it's an inane ritual, and wishing for the same thing for the tenth birthday straight isn't going to make it more likely to happen, but still, I wish. Because you just have to.

He secures the blindfold back around my eyes, and then he feeds me the cupcake. This time it's more intimate. It's not a fork, it's his hand... his finger pressing a bit of the pink buttercream frosting into my mouth. It tastes homemade. Did he make the cupcake, too?

I only worry for a split second that the cupcake is poisoned. But I'm now more concerned about something else. This feels like a seduction. And I don't want to think this thought, I desperately don't. I want to shove it back into the dark pit from which it came, but I can't stop it. His voice is sexy. Like... panty-melting, rough gravel. An auditory fucking orgasm. A throbbing need starts between my legs at this observation.

I am deeply disturbed. I know this. There are no more

excuses now. After killing someone and then just going about my day the next day, and now finding someone who is basically my part-time captor, sexy, I really should be committed somewhere with soft padded walls and a nice calming view of a tree.

I don't even know what he looks like. I do know he's young. Maybe in his thirties? I can tell now that his voice isn't being magnified by a sound system. This psychopath is going to kill me or hurt me, and I'm speculating about how old he is and how hot he may or may not be. Well, now we know. I would have been one of those stupid twits trying to help Ted Bundy.

"Stop thinking so much," he says. "Just enjoy your cupcake."

One might assume that it's only the high-stress situation that makes me not worry a cupcake and lasagna will make me too fat to move across the stage. But that's not true. I mean, sure, I can't eat pasta and sugar every day, but most dancers eat a lot more than you might think. We're burning a ton of calories every day, and we have a lot of muscle that keeps our metabolism revved at a high rate. Most of us eat a normal amount of food. Really, we do. We need the fuel.

A glass prods at my lips, and I find the liquid he poured into the new glass is water. I didn't even get a chance to glance at it while the blindfold was off. My hands are *still* on the table. I haven't moved them since I first placed them there. Because he told me not to, and it's just not worth it to fight him on that, not when he hasn't started doing anything horrific to me yet.

"Don't move until I tell you to move," he says. Then there is more table clearing, something else placed on the table, and then he's gone.

In the silence that follows, the thought occurs to me... if he's really letting me leave this building and carry on with my life for the most part, and I truly believe he's part of the company—which I do—then this is a man I see nearly every day. This is a man I know. At least from a distance. And it must be from a distance because I don't recognize his voice. So one of the principal dancers, or one of the choreographers or instructors who only works with the principals?

Several minutes have passed of me contemplating all this when his voice booms out over the speaker again. "You may take the blindfold off."

I take it off. Sitting in front of me on the table is a black gift bag with gold tissue paper and gold glittery letters on the front that say: "Happy Birthday."

All the dishes and the gun have been taken away. I try to shove away the thought that he has my gun now. I really don't think he's going to shoot me with it. And I haven't died yet from the food. No, he has far grander plans than a quick death for me.

"Open it."

I pull the bag toward me, remove the tissue paper, and take out two large and clearly very expensive bottles of bath oil. The label reads "warm vanilla". I know the principals are paid very well here, but even so, I'm starting to doubt this guy is a principal. I mean, why would he spend this money? What is this guy's game?

"On Wednesdays, before you come to me, I want you to take a bath. Use this oil, rose petals, and candles, and just relax until the heat leaves the water. I'll know if you use the oil by scent and the way your skin feels, but I can't know if you'll do the rest. It will be up to you whether you decide it's worth trying to lie to me, or just obey my orders even when I'm not there."

Another long breath escapes me. It feels like a million

years ago that I was crying, worrying about poisoned lasagna. "Why are you doing this?"

"Does it matter at this point? You are dismissed until Wednesday. When you go out into the lobby, you'll find a key on the counter of the concession stand. Use it to unlock the side door and lock it behind you when you come in each week. We don't want to be disturbed, do we?"

I sit, stunned. I still don't know what he wants from me. *Specifically* what he wants, I mean. I have some ideas, and I'm scared but maybe not as scared as I should be.

Padded wall. Nice calm view of a tree.

"H-how long?" I ask.

"As long as I want. Until I'm done with you."

"And then what?"

"Then nothing."

"You won't report me?"

"If you obey me? No."

"What will you..."

Before I can figure out how to phrase my question, he says, "No more questions. Go home, Ms. Lane. I'll see you Wednesday night at nine."

The spotlight shuts off, and I'm left in darkness. It takes a while for my eyes to adjust, but when they do, I see the darkness isn't total. There are red glowing exit signs, and the floor guide lights, and a few other small out-of-the-way lights I didn't notice before under the overpowering glare of the spotlight. It's just enough for me to see the outline of my things on the stage floor. I gather them up, stuff them in my bag, and leave as quickly as I can, afraid every second that he will grab me, that he will touch me now that his identity is shielded by so much darkness.

But nothing happens. I barely have the presence of mind

to grab the gleaming gold-colored key on the concession stand counter on my way through the lobby. The metal side door clangs and a gust of cool air hits me when I step outside. I run full-out to my car, lock myself inside, and get the fuck out of there.

3

I t's Tuesday night, and I'm exhausted. Part of it is
rehearsals. Part of it is the emotional drain of what I did
the other night, accompanied by last night's introduction to my blackmailer and jailer. It's putting a lot of extra
strain on me, and I'm pretty sure I didn't get more than four
hours' sleep last night.

I spent all day today at rehearsal trying to figure out who
this guy is. The principal dancers cluster together and keep to
themselves, but I need to know if one of the male principals is
my blackmailer. Or is it one of the instructors or choreographers? It's not Mr. V. Obviously. I know his voice. And this guy
is younger.

All day I wondered if my blackmailer was right in front of
me, quietly mocking me.

Henry pops in a DVD, pulling me from my thoughts. The
movie starts. We're sitting in my living room: Me, Henry, and
Melinda.

"Oh God, no, not this one again. I hate this one!" I whine.

"Nope, you have to. It's the start of the season, and we have to watch this movie. It's the ballet movie we all love to hate. It is our forever frenemy," he says.

"It's like a hate fuck," I say.

"YES!" Henry exclaims, shoving a bowl of popcorn onto my lap. "You hate it, but at the same time, it's so good."

I know he brought the DVD to make us watch the bonus features. We're about halfway through the movie when Melinda says "I fucking hate her mother. What is wrong with this woman?"

"Oh, I know!" Henry says.

"Cue fragile emotional meltdown and stereotype of the uptight repressed ballerina," Melinda says, sounding dramatic and distressed.

"Drink!" I say. Because we all drink every time this girl has some meltdown. "Where does that myth even come from? Like bitch, please, try living one day in my life and tell me ballerinas are these delicate fragile flowers about to fall apart every second."

"They do that to the men, too," Henry says.

"Not really in this movie," I say. Which is probably why he likes it. The stereotypes are all on the girls this time.

"I mean in general. Like there is this assumption of weakness in men who dance ballet. And that we're all gay."

"You *are* gay," Melinda says throwing a handful of popcorn at him.

"Yeah, but I'm one of only three out of the whole company! I want a refund. I was sold a lie!"

In spite of the fact that tomorrow is Wednesday and all that may mean, I can't help laughing. I can't help trying to hold onto this moment where everything seems good and normal.

"Besides, the male dancers are always touching the female dancers pretty intimately," Melinda says.

"If we had any other job, and our male co-workers touched us like our partners do for some of these lifts, it would be a sexual harassment scandal," I say a little loud because I always get a little loud when I drink.

By this point, the movie has been drowned out with our rants about dance politics and how non-dancers will never understand us.

"When is Conall coming home?" Melinda asks suddenly, completely killing all the joy in this night—even though she doesn't mean to or even realize she did it.

My mind goes to the grout in the master bathroom. I'm like a hamster in a wheel with this grout issue. And I feel like I've got a guilty look on my face, but we're all drunk and nobody will notice. Right? "He said a few weeks."

"Has he called?"

"He never calls when he's out of town."

"I bet he's with that whore he named the boat after... what's her name again?" Henry asks.

"Stella," I say. "And probably."

"The Delectable Stella," Melinda clarifies, as if this clarification needs to be made. "What kind of piece of shit takes his mistress on a not-so-secret vacation on his wife's birthday? And at the start of the dance season."

"Conall does," I say. "Anyway, I hate for him to watch me perform. He makes me nervous. He doesn't get ballet, and he gets weird about Henry. He thinks we've got something going on."

Henry rolls his eyes. "Must be that magical sexual orientation altering vagina you've got."

I laugh out loud at that and punch him in the arm, causing

him to slosh tequila onto the sofa. I'm glad we're off tomorrow. We all know we can't be drinking like this during performance season. We have to be focused, but it's a last hoorah before everything kicks off. It's not that we never have alcohol or go to parties during the season; we just try to keep it to a minimum. We need to be in top performance condition—like any professional athlete—which is ultimately what we are.

"I don't understand why you're still in the corps," Melinda says. "You're one of the best dancers in the entire company. They're idiots for not promoting you. Who did you piss off?"

I've often wondered the same, but it's nice to hear it from someone else, to know I'm not delusional, thinking I'm better than I truly am.

I WAKE ON WEDNESDAY MORNING WITH A JOLT AND HEART palpitations. It's like my body knows even before I'm fully conscious that I have to go back to the old opera house tonight and confront my blackmailer again. I wish it was money. I wish I could just drop some amount every week in a paper bag and leave it by the back door.

I take several long, slow breaths and try not to cry, but the tears come anyway, sliding down the sides of my face onto my pillow.

What is he going to do to me? Who is he? Is he going to hurt me? And in all honesty what I mean here is: *is he going to hit me*? Is he a violent man? I don't really have the mental real estate right now to berate myself for my physical reaction to that voice. I know I shouldn't have this sick attraction, but a part of me is grateful for it and hope it lasts because that's better than the alternative.

There's already so much that weighs me down that I'm not going to blame myself if some part of me wants this man. I killed my husband, and I don't feel especially guilty about that. So I've pretty much left the realm of normal socially acceptable behavior. I'm already a stranger to the world and to myself. What's one more thing?

But I am afraid he'll hurt me, like Conall hurt me. Kicks and slaps and punches—always in places no one can see the bruises—aren't a theory to me. I know what it feels like, and if this man is going to do those things... if I freed myself from one brutal monster only to be abused by another... would prison be better? I don't know the answer to that. I just want to dance. And I don't understand why that has to be so fucking complicated.

His threat of punishment Monday night surges back into my memory. What does that mean? I know what it meant when Conall did it. Though Conall never said he was going to punish me. He didn't use those words. He just flew into a rage and yelled, and threw things, and hurt me. And he was never calm about it. This man—this stranger—was so calm that even when he used that word, even as my terror climbed, there was a stillness running through me under everything because I could feel the same stillness running through him.

I make bacon and eggs and sit quietly in the kitchen nook staring out the window at the birds crowding around the bird feeder as I eat. Then I try to scrub the grout in the bathroom again. Nothing I do matters though. Not even bleach. I can still see the faint stain of the blood.

Sometimes I think maybe I'm hallucinating it. But it's not as if I can ask someone to come over and tell me if they see the blood, too, or if it's just me.

I finally give up and leave the house. We're lucky to have a huge dance supply warehouse in the city. Yes, people can order stuff online, but some things—as a dancer—you really want to try on. Even if you know your size in a certain brand of leotard, unless the straps are exactly the same and the back is exactly the same, you want to try it on so you can get a feel for how you'll move in it. If something pinches or digs in somewhere, you don't want to spend hours dancing that way.

Trying on shoes is also smart because all the brands and styles are a little different. And I like to try on leg warmers personally because some of them are just way too thick—and then I'm too hot. I like a lighter material—enough to protect joints and muscles until I warm up, but not so much that I have to get rid of them in the middle of class or rehearsal to not feel like I'm going to catch on fire.

I worry the entire drive to the dance warehouse that despite the size of the place they won't have the exact things I've been ordered to wear. But then I reason it's unlikely he'll call the police just because the leotard is the slightly wrong shade or cut. Right? I don't know what this man is capable of or how he defines the word reasonable. A reasonable person wouldn't make any of the demands or threats he's made.

Luckily, this is a wasted fear. Everything he wants is here. I try on and buy several medium gray and several plum-colored leotards with low scooped backs. I grab extra tights while I'm here because you can never have too many pairs of tights. I try on and buy several new pairs of canvas ballet shoes. Mine are falling apart and definitely aren't up to his code.

They have a new line of canvas ballet slippers that a lot of the girls in the company are switching to, and as soon as I slip a pair on, I know why. They hug my foot in exactly the right places, and give me room where I need it, but none where I don't. I can't wait to dance in them.

And even though I have pink leg warmers, I can't resist the siren call of more. And definitely more hip warmers. What the fuck, right? I mean I'm being blackmailed so... it's not like this isn't necessary shopping. It's the first time I've ever mentally defended a shopping binge with *but I'll go to prison if I don't buy it.*

I would probably be tempted to buy more *pointe* shoes if my shoes weren't all custom made for me and provided by the company. I have a hundred and twenty brand new pairs. I know that sounds like obsessive compulsive hoarding behavior, but most professional dancers go through a hundred pairs of *pointe* shoes or more in a season.

After the shopping, I pick up a bouquet of pink roses because I'm not convinced I can believably lie to him when he demands to know if I followed all his instructions. And it's not worth the possible cost.

When I get home, I take off tags and throw everything in the laundry to wash and put the roses in water. I sew my elastics into all my new shoes and try them on again. And then I'm a basket case for the next several hours waiting for my fate to unfold.

At seven p.m., I have dinner. I know it's morbid, but it's leftover lasagna from the other night. I didn't poison the whole pan, just what was on Conall's plate. I wasn't going to waste an entire pan of lasagna on that piece of shit. I just don't have the mental energy right now to cook something else. My mind is too full of what might happen tonight.

After dinner, I put the dishes in the dishwasher, as if this bit of housework is going to slow down the clock. I draw a bath in the oversized garden tub in the master bathroom and pour in the warm vanilla bath oil. I sprinkle the petals from a couple of roses on top of the water and light beeswax candles.

I push play on a swan lake CD and slip into the hot soothing water.

For just a moment I let myself forget about tonight and why I'm taking this ritual bath. I lean back against the edge of the tub and close my eyes. My fingers trail through the water, chasing rose petals around the tub.

When the water turns cool, I hop in the shower to wash my hair. By the time my hair is in a bun, and I'm dressed according to his dress code, it's already eight-thirty.

4

I t's a few minutes after nine when I arrive at the opera house. I fumble with the key to get in the side door and rush into the theater. I don't have time to be afraid about what I'm doing or to think too hard on it because I'm late.

"You're late, Ms. Lane," the voice says over the sound system, filling the theater with its demands.

"I'm sorry. There was traffic."

"There's always traffic. I expect you here at nine. You are stealing time from me. You know how to be on time, Ms. Lane. I know you do. Are you late to rehearsals? Classes?"

He's not yelling at me but his voice is so hard right now, and part of me wants to run out of here before this starts— before he hurts me.

"No, Sir," I say. I can already feel the tears sliding down my face. I don't know what exactly I'm crying about, but he makes me feel like I'm the worst person in the world for being five minutes late to the appointment of being his slave for three hours.

"You will remain five extra minutes to make up for it. Go to the barre and warm up."

When I get on the stage, I peel off my outer layer of clothing and run my hand over my hair to make sure no stray strands have fallen out. I put on my soft ballet shoes, hip warmers, and leg warmers, and I go to the barre. I see that the blindfold is draped over the edge, and my breath hitches in my throat.

Music begins to play over the sound system. Swan Lake. Does he get a perverse thrill out of reminding me he knows everything about my life, my world, my schedule? He knows when I'm in class. He knows which ballet we're working on. He knows everything. And he doesn't seem to miss an opportunity to remind me of it.

I still don't understand this. I mean sure, if he just wanted to fuck me it would make some kind of sense. If he wanted money, that would make sense, too. But what is he getting out of watching me warm up at the barre? I roll my eyes at myself, realizing I've answered my own question.

Maybe he *does* get off on it. Maybe he's turned on by watching dancers. That isn't a rare fetish after all. For all I know, he's jerking off right now. Who *is* this guy?

I spend about fifteen minutes running through my full warm-up routine, surprised when he doesn't interrupt me. Then I do some stretches at the barre and on the floor. When I'm finished, I stand, and wait for more instruction.

During these past few minutes, I've somehow been able to mostly block out why I'm here. Because I'm on a stage in a spotlight. I'm at a barre. This is all comforting and familiar even though I shouldn't feel comforted right now.

"I want to see your *grand jetés,*" he says

"I... why? Why are we doing this? I don't understand..."

"Because I own you. I own your body for three hours a week, and right now I want to watch you leap across the stage. Can you manage that, Ms. Lane?"

"Y-yes, Sir."

"Good. Do it then."

I move to one end of the dance floor, take a few graceful dancer runs, and leap across the stage.

"Again."

I do it again. And again.

"Stop," he says. "Take a few minutes and get some water."

I notice for the first time that there's a water bottle on the long rectangular table and am grateful for it. I don't know what I thought I'd be doing for three hours in this theater. I guess I thought something dirty and sexual. I didn't actually think I'd be dancing, like... training.

Am I disappointed about this? Did I want his hands on me? I think back to his finger pressing the pink buttercream frosting into my mouth. God help me, but... maybe.

When I return, he says, "Your *grand jeté* could go higher. You have the proper training and strength, but you're pulling your jump back before you even get in the air. Think of it like a rocket launch. You need a deeper *plié* going into the jump, and all the proper muscles need to fire at the right time. It's an explosion of movement. If you can remember and apply that, you should get more lift and also move farther across the stage with it. And don't try to use your shoulders to jump. Try again, please."

He just corrected me. And I can't help this twisted happiness about that. In ballet, you learn to take corrections as compliments because the truth is, most instructors won't waste their time on trying to make you better if they don't think you're capable. So even though this man is holding threats over my head, and it's not like we mutually agreed to do some outside-of-class practice sessions, I can't shut off years and years of training and the flush of pleasure corrections give me.

I go back to the edge of the stage, think through all the things he just told me, and then implement the correction.

"Good girl," he says. "I want to see it one more time from the other direction."

I do it again from the other direction, my mind scurrying like a helpless mouse back and forth over that *Good girl*. What the fuck? We may hear "Good", in class, but no ballet teacher says "Good girl" like that.

When I stop and wait for more direction, he says, "Do you know why you aren't a principal?"

I brace myself for some insult about how I just don't have *it*. Whatever *it* is. "No, Sir," I say.

I know from his correction that this man knows dance. He's been in this world a long time, so he probably *does* know why I'm not a principal. And I desperately do not want to hear it. I don't want to hear that there is no hope for me. I want to believe Melinda and Henry's opinions that I'm the best—that there's something wrong with the decision makers at the company, not something wrong with me.

"The company was struggling financially until your husband started making very generous donations. At first, they thought he was trying to buy you a principal role. But that wasn't what he was doing. He said: 'Keep her in the corps. She can have the occasional small solo, but nothing more. And if you want the money to keep flowing, she never hears of this.' That's why you aren't a principal. It's nothing to do with you or your talent or dedication. It's business."

I grip the barre for support, shaken by this revelation. Conall and I fought over and over about dance, about how much time the company took away from him, about my dance partner, about everything. He was jealous of my relationship with the stage, but it never occurred to me that he'd do something like this. He'd seemed like my savior when I met him, someone who could give me comfort and security and let me follow my dreams to dance without the near-poverty that often goes with this career choice.

I thought I was winning—even when he became so possessive and angry all the time. Even when he got violent. I still somehow thought I was lucky.

The stranger continues, "Conall obviously won't be donating anymore, but that's okay. I can match and exceed his donation. I had planned to do that anyway. Prove to me you can be a principal, and I will elevate you."

I stand in stunned silence. Why is my blackmailer handing me everything I want? There's a catch. I know there's a catch.

"You want me to fuck you for a promotion?" I ask, a flutter of unwanted excitement in my stomach.

"Language, Ms. Lane. You know dancers don't speak that way in rehearsal or a class environment."

"I'm sorry, Sir. Is that your price? For a promotion? Sex?" Because honestly, I might happily pay it.

He laughs. "No, Cassia. You will fuck me with or without the promotion. I'll see to it that you're promoted because you're the brightest rising star in this company, and I'll get zero push back when I insist on it. Now go back to the barre, and put the blindfold on."

Suddenly the fear is back again because I know the blindfold means he's leaving his hidden perch and coming into my space. My mental bravado about how I would probably happily fuck him is replaced again by anxiety as I tie the blindfold around my eyes.

Then I wait.

I feel him before I hear his footsteps or his voice. His presence is so palpable that I'm not sure this man could sneak up on me if he tried. I can tell he's a few feet away when he speaks again.

"First position, two *demi-pliés*, one *grand plié* with the standard arm movements you use in class, then a *port de bras* forward and back"

I hear a tiny click, and music begins to play. It's beyond strange doing this blindfolded, but my free hand rests on the barre, and I've done this so many thousands of times that I don't need to see anything. I move fluidly through the exercise. When I bend forward in the *port de bras* my fingertips graze the dance tarp beneath my feet, and I sweep my arm back up.

When I arch my back, my arm going with the movement, that's when he touches me. His large hand encircles my wrist, gently stroking the pulse point, and I gasp. It feels as though something electric passed from him all the way through me from that simple touch.

The music stops.

I feel the strength in his hand even though he isn't gripping me hard. The way he touches me reminds me just how small I am, how tiny my wrists, how absolutely breakable. He could snap any bone in my body in half with no effort at all.

Before I can dwell on this thought, his hand leaves my wrist and skims down my back until he's touching the back of my hips with one hand and the front of my hips with the other. His hands are placed so intimately on my body I can barely breathe.

But it's not a sexual touch. It's a normal touch for correcting a body position. Intimate, yes, but still normal for me. His hand spans my hips completely, his wrist grazing one hip bone, while his fingertips rest against the other.

"Such a beautiful turnout," he murmurs.

There's a long beat of silence while he holds me in this position, his hands warming against me while the weight of the absolute imbalance of power between us settles on me in a way it couldn't before. There was no space for it before. No silence. But the way he holds me in place... the subtle way he lets me know my new reality through this gentle touch... tells me everything.

He leans in close. "You *want* me to fuck you, don't you?" He practically growls these words in my ear.

"Y-yes, Sir." I whimper. I've never been in such close proximity to someone who could make me feel so much sexual need so easily. I'm getting so wet for him with almost no provocation. It's embarrassing.

I do want him. I don't care how fucked up this is. It isn't the power he has to promote me—if he's not lying about that—or the power he has to destroy me, whether in his physical strength or by a simple call to the police. I *viscerally* want this man.

I've never wanted someone so completely in such an animal magnetic way. He takes his hands off my hips, and I almost beg him to put them back. I need his hands on me. The list of reasons I'm crazy just keeps getting bigger with every second I fall into this seduction.

This man is evil. If he would blackmail me like this... I don't even know who he is. He could be anybody. But I don't care. I don't care. *Please please please touch me again.*

As if hearing my silent prayer, his fingertips brush against my nipples, which harden instantly against the fabric of my leotard. Maybe they were already erect. I can't think. I've never felt so out of control of my own body's reactions. He takes my wrist again and brings my arm down into a low resting position in front of me.

He moves into my space even more. I almost flinch away even as I want to lean into him. His mouth presses against my throat in a devouring kiss. Then he pulls away.

"I will fuck you soon, but not tonight." It's a promise, practically a vow.

Then he leans in again and smells my neck. "Good, you used the bath oil. Did you follow the rest of my orders? Rose petals and candles? Soak until the bath goes cool?"

"Yes, Sir," I whisper.

There's a pause, a long pregnant silence, as though he's assessing the truth of my words. "Good girl," he finally says.

I feel him move away from me then. And I wait. I stand exactly as he placed me, and I wait. I want to cry. I want to fall to my knees and beg this man to fuck me. The need for him is so primal, so consuming that nothing else matters. No, I'm not scared he'll fuck me. I'm scared he won't. I'm scared that along with whatever other mind games he designs for me, that he will lead me on and tease and torment me, but never let me experience the bliss of his body inside mine.

A few minutes pass like this, then his voice comes out of the speaker again. "Remove the blindfold and go to the center," he says as if nothing happened. As if he never left his hiding place. And for a moment, some hysterical part of me thinks everything that just happened was all my imagination.

I step away from the barre, shaky and flustered. I feel the warm wetness surging between my legs. He leaves me desperate and wanting, craving. He's all business now. For the rest of our time together, he runs me through my corps choreography for Swan Lake—all except for the parts I dance with Henry.

"That's enough for tonight. Go backstage to the dressing rooms. Take a shower, change back into your street clothes, and come back to the stage."

I'm a bit surprised by this order. I thought he'd work me until the very last second when he promised to release me, but a hot shower sounds really fucking good right now. I go backstage. He's left me a trail of lights along the hallways, through the dressing rooms, all the way back to the shower.

The bathroom has been newly renovated. So work *has* been done on this place. Everything is clean white tile and sleek steel lines for the counters. Fresh pale blue towels wait for me on an elegant slatted wooden bench—like something you might see in a spa. There's lavender soap in the shower.

I look around, half afraid and half hoping he'll come in while I'm undressing, but I know he won't. He won't let me see him. I look up to find a small black camera in the corner of the ceiling, angled down over the shower. Is he sitting in a control room where he can observe the screen I'm on? Is he touching himself?

I swallow hard, but I strip off my dance clothes, free my hair from the bun, and step into the shower. I feel his eyes on me through the camera lens. I half expect his voice to sound through a speaker in here as well with a new list of demands, but it doesn't. The only sound is the spray of the shower. Here I'm allowed both the sweet privacy and relentless torment of my own thoughts.

I clean up quickly, use one of the towels to dry off, and change into my street clothes. My hair is wet and flowing past my shoulders. I put my things back in my dance bag and return to the stage, like a *good girl*. I don't stand on the black tarp. Not in my street shoes. I would never.

"Homework," he says over the speaker. "I want you to learn Odette's first solo in Swan Lake as well as the first *pas de deux*."

"I need a partner for that."

"Just learn what you can," he says. "You're dismissed. Be ready to work on it next week."

Once again, the lights go out, and I'm left in darkness and confusion.

It's opening night of Swan Lake. Every time I'm on stage with the rest of the corps, I feel his gaze on me. I wonder if I'm paranoid. Maybe I'm losing it. How do I feel him so strongly? How could I possibly know he's out there, watching me? I miss one small step in the second act, and somehow I know he saw it.

It's such a small mistake. No one who doesn't know exactly what the choreography should be would know. And they would have to be watching my feet specifically. But I know he saw. And I'm suddenly seized with an irrational fear about this. I somehow make it through the performance with that mistake gnawing at the back of my mind the entire time.

While we're all out on stage taking our bows, I look up to the box seats. There is a man in the front box closest to the stage on my left. He's by himself, no date. That alone makes me believe it's him. There aren't many men who would attend the ballet alone.

He's tall and broad, in a suit. But that's all I can make out—and only just barely. His face—in fact his whole body—is cast in shadow. I can tell he's standing, clapping with the rest of the audience as Natalie and Frederick come out onto the stage to take their bows, but somehow I know he's not watching them. I feel his gaze on me.

After the performance, the dancers go out for drinks. The principals keep to themselves at their own private table, while those in the corps hang out at the bar. At least half of us drink club soda. We have another performance tomorrow night, so we can't get drunk. And we've got too much adrenaline going to want to dampen it with alcohol. Opening night is the best night in the world.

Henry and Melinda sit on either side of me abuzz with excitement, rambling on about how well they think it went. But I barely hear their words. I leave early, feeling exhausted, but once I get home, I can't sleep. I have to know who was sitting in that box.

On Friday, I go to the box office. My friend Lilah works there, managing ticket sales for all the ballets.

"Hey, girl! I caught opening night. You guys were great!" she says, glancing up from her computer.

"Thanks."

An office door opens, and a man steps out. "Lilah, I'm going to lunch," he says.

"Okay, Mr. Simmons."

His eyes sweep over me like he thinks I'll keep her from her work. And I swear even though I just heard his voice and know it's not *him*, the way he looks at me makes me feel like this is the guy. It seems like he'll ask me to leave, but he just turns and walks out the glass door into the main lobby. Once he's out of the building, I turn back to Lilah.

"Listen," I say, "I was wondering if you could tell me who was in one of the private boxes at last night's performance."

"You know I can't share that. The ticket holder information

is kept in the strictest of confidence. Most of our patrons are well-off and take their privacy very seriously."

It sounds like she's quoting an employee training video. I expect her to plaster on a fake too-stretched smile and announce how happy she is to be part of the Tivoli theater family.

"Lilah... come on... I really need to know... I'm not going to say anything to anyone."

She looks around again, as if confirming that her boss really has left, that he didn't forget something and slip back inside to catch her break this most sacred of security oaths. She finally sighs. "Okay."

She motions for me to join her. I go behind the counter so I can see the screen as she types.

"Which box was it?"

"The one closest to the stage."

"Right or left?"

"It was my left when I was looking out at the audience."

She types. I wait. A screen pops up which should give us a name, but instead it says: "Season ticket holder. Private. Reserved."

"That's weird," she says. She clicks onto something else, but the screen locks her out. "We always have to have their information on file in the system. Always."

"Thanks anyway."

Lilah gives me an apologetic smile, but I shrug, act like it's no big deal, and leave, even more sure it's him and not just my imagination.

5

I'm sure he watched me all four nights from that private box nearest the stage. I felt him. I didn't make any more mistakes the rest of the performances, so maybe if he noticed the one on opening night, he won't comment the next time I see him.

On Monday I've got a free period while the principals are rehearsing. Natalie, Frederick, and Mr. V are running some of the choreography in Studio A, which is the largest rehearsal space. There's an extra mirror at the far end of the studio and several barres set up where other dancers—mostly from the corps—are using this time to warm up and rehearse some of their own parts.

I take a spot at the end of one of the barres and put my *pointe* shoes on. But I don't practice my own steps. I'm watching Natalie. She's going through Odette's opening solo piece. It feels like I've seen this a thousand times, so on a certain level I know it already. But my feet don't know it like my brain does.

I stand off to the side and mimic her movements. It's the

same Swan Lake choreography we've used since I've been here, so it's easy to pick up—easier than I thought it would be. I glance over to find Mr. V. has stopped watching Natalie.

Instead, he's watching me. Natalie doesn't notice. She's too wrapped up in her role as Odette. I shift my focus back to her and continue marking and learning the steps, but I feel Mr. V.'s eyes on me.

When the music stops he says, "Take five and get some water, then we'll work with Frederick on the *pas de deux*."

As soon as Natalie has gone off to follow his direction, he makes a beeline across the floor to me. He's so intense that several other dancers nearby stop what they're doing to watch.

"May I see you privately out in the hallway?" he asks, his voice low and curt.

I just nod and follow him out of the studio, my stomach going into a tight hard knot with each step. The hallway is empty. All the dancers are in either Studio A or B working on something for the show.

"What were you doing in there?" he asks, keeping his voice low. "You aren't the understudy. We've already set the list for the season. You're distracting me."

For a moment, I just stand there staring at him, the nervous dread gone now that he's said this out loud. How am I distracting him? I'm off in the corner doing what I'm doing. It's not as though I'm dancing in front of Natalie right in his face screaming for his attention.

"I-I'm sorry. I know. I just wanted a challenge... to learn more." It's not as if I can tell him the real reason. *It's blackmail homework to stay out of prison* would require a much longer explanation. One I'm not prepared to give.

Mr. V. sighs. I can actually see the pity on his face. And then I know. My mysterious blackmailer was telling the truth.

Conall really was keeping me from progressing in the company. I could have been a principal.

"Go get some lunch and meet me in the small studio at two p.m. I have a couple of hours free on Monday afternoons."

"I... wait what?"

"I'm going to work with you, Ms. Lane. You did say you want to learn and be challenged, right?"

"Yes! Thank you!" I think I squeal this. I know I hug him. Then I quickly step back and practically flee from the building before he can change his mind.

I grab lunch at a nearby cafe and am back in the small studio warming up at the barre by one-thirty. The small studio is the third studio space in the building. It really is a small and intimate space, but it's large enough for a couple of dancers to rehearse when the other spaces are being used. And it's private to keep out distractions.

There are a few other small rooms that can be used for this purpose as well, but the small studio is the only one with proper sprung floors, a barre, a mirror, and a CD player for music.

We have live accompaniment in the bigger studios.

Mr. V. walks in right at two o'clock. "I'll need a few minutes," he says, sitting down at a table in the corner and unpacking a lunch of his own.

I stretch some more and wait while he eats.

"What were you wanting to learn?" he asks, in between bites of a chicken salad sandwich he picked up from the same cafe I just returned from. I should have asked if he wanted me to get his lunch. If this is more than just a one-time pity session, I'll pick his food up for him next time.

"The first solo and the first *pas de deux*." I say it more like it's a question than a statement because I know just how presumptuous it sounds.

We both know I need a partner for the *pas de deux*. And while he may for some reason be feeling generous with me, he's not going to pull Frederick or his understudy away to engage in fruitless practice that won't turn into anything. It would raise weird questions. *This* will probably raise weird questions—the fact that he's even in this private studio space with me at all.

Mr. V. doesn't comment on this. He just eats the rest of his sandwich and drinks his iced tea. "All right," he finally says. I'm not sure if he's agreeing to my syllabus or if he's merely stating that he's ready to begin.

I stand, and he stands. I'm surprised when he opens his bag and takes out a pair of his own ballet shoes and puts them on. He does a few warm-up exercises and stretches at the barre. He's been retired from the Bolshoi for ten years, but he doesn't move like someone retired for a decade. He moves as though he performed with us yesterday. It makes me suddenly wonder if he still dances for himself in his off time. Maybe he has a barre at home like I do.

Mr. V. spends the first hour teaching me the solo. It's easy to pick up because I've seen it so many times. But since I've seen it in rehearsals and not on stage, there are a few parts I've missed. He spends extra time on those parts, making sure I have it down before moving on.

He plays the music and lets me do the entire solo once I know all the parts. He shouts out a couple of corrections as I go. I fix them on the next run through.

"Very good," he says. "We've got another hour. I'll teach you the *pas de deux*."

"I need a partner."

"It's been a while, but I think I can manage," Mr. V. says.

I worry I've offended him, but when I look up, he's smiling at me.

"Okay," I say.

He's still an amazing dancer. So much better than Henry, though I will never ever tell Henry that. It would hurt him even though he knows he'll never get out of the corps. He's a solid corps dancer, but he's not principal material. As far as I can tell, he doesn't seem sad about this. He accepted the truth of it long ago.

"Do you miss it?" I ask Mr. V. when we finish for the day. Another rehearsal is starting in Studio B, and both of us need to be in there.

"Sometimes," he says. "But I also love teaching. Two p.m. next week?"

"Yes." This time I manage to contain my squeals and hugs.

By the time Wednesday night rolls around, I've practiced Odette's solo more times than I can count in my private studio space at home, and I've done what little I can of the *pas de deux* alone, marking all of the parts as well as I can.

I'm wearing the plum leotard today and all the other things he requested.

"I want you *en pointe* tonight," the voice says over the speaker system.

I strip off my outer layer of clothes, finish getting ready, and put my *pointe* shoes on. I pull on my leg warmers and stand at the barre to begin my warmups. I want to ask if he was at the show opening night, but before I can find a way to phrase the question, he speaks again.

"I saw the mistake Thursday night. I'm sure no one else noticed it, but I noticed it."

I swallow hard. He doesn't say anything else. I'm finished with my warm-ups before he speaks again.

"I want to see the solo, now."

I move to the center of the stage. When the music begins I do the solo exactly as Mr. V. taught it to me. When the music stops, I stand there, pleased with myself, sure I've impressed him.

"The angle of your *arabesque* is off. And your second turn could have been tighter. Try again."

I'm sure I did this exactly as I was taught. But thinking on it, the angle was a little off, and maybe the turn could have been tighter. This man is pickier than Mr. V. But I only nod.

"Speak," he says, as though training a dog.

"Yes, Sir," I say, rattled.

The music starts again. This time I get it right, and I can feel his pleasure at my performance.

"Beautiful. Go to the barre and put the blindfold on."

I'm sure that as long as he makes me come to him every week like this, the order to put the blindfold on will make me feel this way—this unbalanced nervous energy in my stomach. It's fear and excitement... anticipation. He's coming to me. What will he do? Will he touch me? Will he fuck me? His promise of *soon* has played all week on repeat in my mind like a background soundtrack to my life.

I stand at the barre, the blindfold in place, trying to calm my breathing. Again, I feel his approach before I hear it.

"Face the barre, and bend forward into a parallel stretch."

I do as he asks, and a moment later, there's a hard slap against my ass. I gasp. My instinct is to take my hands from the barre to rub the sting out.

"Do *not* move your hands," he says, as though reading my mind.

I stay perfectly still, waiting for the sting to fade.

"That was for your error on Thursday. Don't do it again, or I'll punish you. Now stand upright."

I do as he asks, trying to process what just happened. I feel the heat in my face, knowing he sees my blush. He *spanked* me. Like some misbehaving child, for a minor misstep onstage. I know, given my violent history with Conall, I should rip the blindfold off and try to run. But for some reason, I'm not scared. Even though he just smacked my ass, it's not the same.

Everything he says, everything he does is nothing but control. Nothing is erratic or impulsive. It feels somehow safe. Conall was never in control.

"Did you learn the *pas de deux*?" he asks as if that didn't just happen.

"Yes, Sir. Mr. V. taught me. He danced it with me."

He chuckles. "Did he? And how was that?"

"He's an incredible dancer."

"He is. I caught one of his last performances with the Bolshoi years ago. Are you ready?"

"Ready for what?"

"To do the *pas de deux*," he says as if this is the stupidest question I could possibly ask.

"I can't do it without a partner. Or... blindfolded. I can't dance blindfolded."

Then he's there, right next to me, his warm breath in my ear. "Yes. You can. I won't let you fall off the stage. Just trust me."

Trust him? I almost laugh out loud at that. As if I could ever trust this man. I push down the traitorous voice in my mind that says I already do trust him... a little.

He takes my hand and guides me around the stage to each of the marks we'll hit during the *pas de deux*, talking me through each piece of the choreography, then he leads me back to the center of the stage, turns me toward what I imagine must be the audience—or where they would be if this were a real performance.

"Head up, Ms. Lane. Never forget you are on a stage."

The music starts. And then his hands are on me. He dances the *pas de deux* with me. I *can* do this blindfolded, which is truly the weirdest thing to realize.

His hands are nearly always on me in this piece. He's always guiding me, steadying me, lifting me, or turning me. But he's always there. I'm sure now he must be a principal. But if he's a principal, how does he have box seats for the season? He's not in Swan Lake. But then not every principal at the company is in this show. But then I'm back to, how does he know this choreography then?

He's good. *Really* good. Better even than Mr. V. This is the best dancer I've ever partnered with. The fluidity of every movement, the certainty of each lift, each touch is exhilarating. His hands are large, strong. I feel like a fragile captive bird in his hands.

I'm suddenly thinking more about all of this than I am about the choreography. I stumble, but he catches me. I half expect him to spank me again, but he doesn't. He just cradles me in his arms.

"I told you I wouldn't let you fall." He sweeps me up. We jump right back into the place where the music is, a few steps forgotten in the wake of my misstep. We dance as though that didn't happen, as if this is all perfect.

The *pas de deux* ends in an embrace. I'm dipped back. He's holding me. The music stops. And there is silence. He pulls me up to stand, facing him, even though I can't see him. Will he touch me? Will he kiss me? One of his hands is at my waist, holding me still in this embrace.

In this strangely tender moment, I reach up to touch his face, but his grip on my wrist is instantaneous, hard, and unrelenting. A silent understanding passes between us in that touch. I'm here to obey, not initiate, not make up my own choreography. I am to perform the steps as they are given. This rule extends beyond dancing.

"I-I'm sorry," I say. I've clearly displeased him somehow, and it bothers me more than I want to admit. I want to say it's because he could report my crime, but some deeper betraying part of me is simply upset I've displeased him. Even if there were no threat over my head... I would come back here because I need to dance with this man. I've never felt this kind of electric chemistry with anyone on stage before.

"Go to the barre," he says.

Absently, I reach up to remove the blindfold, not thinking. But he again grabs my wrist before I can complete the act. He leads me over to the barre and places my hand on the smooth wood. I both feel and hear him move away. He's rifling through my dance bag at the far end of the stage beside the table.

When he returns, I feel his hand on my thigh. He slowly strokes downward until he reaches my ankle. He begins to untie the ribbons of my *pointe* shoes. This is when I realize he must be sitting on the floor beside me. He's silent as he removes first one, then the other. He replaces them with my new pair of soft canvas ballet slippers.

He stands and steps back. Finally, he speaks.

"First position. Two *demi-plié*, one *grand plié*. Then I want you to go from that position into a kneeling position, keeping your legs spread and your hand on the barre."

My breath hitches. And so it begins. This thing I knew was coming. This sexual price he wishes to extract from my body which right now is far more willing to pay than I ever expected it to be.

The music starts, a different piece. It's not from one of our ballets, but piano practice music often used for barre work.

I rest one hand lightly on the barre, not gripping it for support, only for balance. My other arm gracefully sweeps inward as I lower my body into a *demi-plié*. It's a gentle movement, not very deep. And then the second. My heart hammers in my chest as I think about what may happen in the next few moments. But I shove those thoughts away and concentrate on the movement.

The *grand plié* is much deeper, lower to the floor. And then from there, I let myself fall into the kneeling position he asked for, my hand still stretched up, holding onto the barre.

The music fades out. And there is silence.

"Who owns you, Cassia?"

"You, Sir." I don't hesitate to give him this truth.

"Do you wax or shave your pussy?"

This may seem like a huge assumption on his part—that I do either—but most ballet dancers I know keep bare. Our leotards are so revealing—and costumes as well—that most of us want everything to remain smooth.

"Wax," I say.

"Good. That's my preference."

Excitement throbs between my legs. I shouldn't care what his preference is, but the fact that what I do is what he wants makes the place between my legs ache with need for him to possess this thing that has pleased him.

"When is your next waxing appointment?"

"In two weeks."

"You will cancel it. I will be waxing you from now on. Do you understand?"

I can't think. I can barely make the words form, but I force them out because it pleases him to hear them. "Yes, Sir."

I hear a zipper. He strokes my cheek in a mirror of what I attempted to do to him only moments ago.

"Now, Ms. Lane. You will open your mouth and accept me."

His cock prods at my lips.

An erect cock is all rigid hardness with soft skin on top, but the softness is far softer than I remember, experiencing it now without the ability to see or have any distractions from the tactile sensation. I open my mouth, and he slides inside.

The way he's spoken to me from the moment I've met this stranger should make me angry. I should be offended or at the very least scared. But that voice. Those demands. The way he says these things... It all has a purely erotic effect on my body.

I'm so wet right now that he could slide into more than just my mouth without the slightest resistance. But that isn't what he wants in this moment. What he wants is me kneeling blindfolded and helpless at his feet, *accepting him.*

"Good girl."

He's so gentle with me. He is large and hard and thick. The scent of his body makes me want to mount him like a bitch in heat. His hand is at the nape of my neck, guiding but not forcing as I mouth him, kiss him, lick him, suck and stroke him with my free hand. I can feel how close he is with the hardening grip on my neck. He's thrusting inside my mouth, and I accept him, taking him deep into my throat.

His other hand covers mine on the barre as though we're lovers holding hands in a much more innocent situation.

He comes, and I swallow. It doesn't occur to me to do

anything else even though I've never been that girl who swallows. I am that girl right now.

He pulls away, zips up. I feel bereft for a moment. I'm so wet and needing right now. I need him. I need him to touch me. He moves behind me, and his hands are on me.

I'm still kneeling, still holding onto the barre with one hand. I need to hold onto something, so I'm not sure if my hand still on the barre is obedience or necessity. He strokes my breasts over my leotard, and then his hand is grinding between my parted thighs. He's on the ground with me, pulling me back, my body flush against his chest as he touches me.

This goes on for a few moments, then he stops and gets up.

"No! Please... please..." I whimper. He can't stop. Why the fuck is he stopping? I know this is not the question I should ask. If I were a good person, if I were a decent or sane person, I would be relieved by this merciful cessation of his hungry hands devouring my body. But I am not a good person. How can I hold onto that myth any longer in light of the harsh relentless truth between my legs?

"Please what?" he asks, his voice hard again. And I can feel his distance from me. He's too far away for me to touch even if I reached out. And I want to reach out. I want to beg for him. I want to crawl.

"Sir, please... please... don't stop. Please."

I'm still holding onto the barre. My arm is aching, but I can't bring myself to break the position he ordered me into. Mercifully, he takes that hand in his, and pulls me to stand. Then he leads me away somewhere. Off the stage... backstage... I don't know where we're going, but I don't protest.

When we reach the bathroom backstage, I know that's where we are. I feel the tile floor through my soft ballet shoes.

I hear the water go on in the shower. A zipper. Clothing hitting the floor. Then he's stripping me. First the shoes, then the leotard and tights. But the blindfold remains in place. The glass door slides open, and he pulls me into the enveloping wet warmth with him.

I know he's seen me naked before on the screen, but realizing his closeness, feeling the hard naked length of his body pressed against mine is another thing. He's so tall and strong. So much stronger than me. Suddenly being in this confined space with water pouring down on me, naked with a stranger —with my blackmailer—jars me out of his seductive spell.

He could rape me. He could fucking drown me. He could tilt me back and hold his hand over my mouth and just let the water take me. I panic, and then tears come. I'm so isolated from the rest of the world, from anyone who could help or hear me. Suddenly being this vulnerable with this man I don't know scares me in a way I haven't been scared since the note in my locker.

"Shhhh," he says. "Shhh. You're safe." He pulls me into his arms, which should feel more confining, more terrifying, but I can feel his steady heartbeat against my skin, and he's stroking my back in the most delightfully soothing way. I shouldn't melt into him like I do. I shouldn't feel this sense of trust flow out of me and into him. Especially not after Conall. This is a dangerous man. This is not a romantic comedy. This is something dark and disturbing and wrong.

But my brain can't process that reality anymore because he's being so gentle. My arms go around him, clinging to him, my head pressed against his chest, sighing like a contented house cat as he strokes the back of my neck.

"I think that's enough for tonight," he says.

I want to say no. He can't leave me wanting. Even as he says these words, the desire comes flooding back, overriding all doubts and fears. I grip him harder, as if I can stop him from pulling away.

His mouth grazes my ear. "Do you want more?"

"Yes, Sir." I am nothing but adrenaline. Fear and desire blending together until I don't know where one thing ends and the other begins. But I need him to keep touching me.

"Turn around and put your hands on the wall." He doesn't say it in the same hard way as usual. And it doesn't come out in a growl. The command is soft, calm.

And suddenly I am soft, calm.

I do as he says, and a few moments later he's washing me, lathering my body, the relaxing scent of lavender permeating the space.

"I'm going to remove the blindfold. Stay facing the wall, and keep your eyes closed. I really don't want to punish you right now. Do you understand?"

"Yes, Sir." It's barely more than a whisper. But he hears me.

He removes the fabric from my eyes, which has miraculously mostly remained dry, since my face wasn't in the water. Then he releases my hair from the bun. He runs his fingers through it. He shampoos my hair and washes my body, and I stand there, obeying him—my eyes closed, turned toward the shower wall, my hands flat against the tile.

Why the hell am I doing this?

"Good girl," he murmurs in my ear as if it's the answer to my internal questioning.

His hands stroke over my breasts, lingering there. He lingers in this same way on my ass. And then, finally, he's stroking the bare flesh between my thighs, rubbing soothing circles over my clit with one hand as he uses the other to penetrate me. My body begins to move and grind with his thrusting and rubbing fingers.

Desperate vocalizations escape me. Whimpers, moans. Moans that turn to loud, erupting screams of pleasure as he draws the orgasm out of my body. He shatters me and puts me back together as he touches me. He won't relent. He won't stop. He continues until my body can't take anymore. Until my arms and legs are trembling. Until I'm crying from the intensity of it all.

"Shhhh," he whispers in my ear, as he removes his hands. "I'm going to let you go early tonight. You need time and space to process this. This week, I want you to masturbate to orgasm every night. And I want you to think about what happened tonight while you do it. I want you to make those delicious sounds when you come alone in your bed. I'm going to leave now. Don't open your eyes or leave this shower until you're sure I'm gone."

The shower door opens, and I hear him step out. I hear him dressing. I hear him leave. I stand in the shower, my head pressed against the tile. I wait. I have never felt this much pleasure with a man before in my life. I've never wanted like this

I take a deep breath, turn the water off, and step out of the shower. I look up at the camera when I get out, wondering if he's watching me on the monitor. I wonder if he can see the fear in my eyes. I'm afraid of what I feel, afraid of what I want, afraid of this dark slithering thing he's awakened inside of me.

6

Yesterday Mr. V. taught me more in the small private studio. People are beginning to notice this attention he lavishes upon me. There are whispers when I pass in the hall. There are questions. Are we having an affair? What are we doing in that studio for two hours?

I swear if Mr. V's voice wasn't older and so much different from the stranger in the abandoned opera house, if his dancing style weren't so different, I would be sure it must be the same man. There's nothing sexual in Mr. V.'s manner, but his sudden interest in me is just as intense—even if channeled in an entirely different way.

I'm pondering all this as I pass by Mr. V.'s office. The door is partly opened and there's a man with dark hair facing away from the door, staring out the window at the view of the city. The man is tall, broad, athletic. Even though I can't see his face, I know he's beautiful. A new dancer?

Then he speaks. "I'll be here for the board meeting tomorrow afternoon. We can discuss it then."

That voice. It's him. I move closer to the door. Has he

already been discussing me with Mr. V.? Is that why the ballet master started teaching me more? Does Mr. V. know what's happening? No, that doesn't seem right. But I could confide in him. I could tell him this man is hurting me.

But *is* this man hurting me? I'm so confused. I don't know what to think anymore. If I speak up, nothing will stop him from revealing my crime and ruining my life. More importantly, if I speak up, everything ends. And I'm not sure I want it to end. And now, seeing the smallest glimmer of his sheer physicality... it's even harder to want to break away from this beauty.

I've felt him against me. I could have guessed. But to see it is something different.

Turn around. I silently beg. I need to know who this man is. Would I recognize him?

Mr. V. is suddenly standing in the doorway. "Can I help you, Ms. Lane?"

I look over his shoulder and see the other man's body go rigid. I'm supposed to be in Studio A right now, and I'm sure he knows that. One of the choreographers is in there working with the company, but I'm not in that part, so I slipped out to get some air.

Mr. V.'s stare is dark and inscrutable. And his question is obviously rhetorical because he doesn't wait for me to answer him. He simply shuts the door and locks it. The blinds to the window facing out into the hallway shut in a sharp snap of disapproval.

I return to rehearsal, trying not to think about who is in Mr. V.'s office, how well Mr. V. might know him, and what, if anything, I can or should do about this new knowledge.

When we break for lunch, I knock on Mr. V.'s now open door.

"Yes?" he asks, looking up from a pile of papers on his desk.

I scan the room, searching for any sort of evidence from the earlier meeting that may have been left behind. But there is no glaring sign with my blackmailer's photo and name on it anywhere.

"W-who was that man in your office earlier?"

"He is our most generous benefactor. He wishes to remain anonymous." Mr. V.'s eyes hold a challenge. He stares me down like an alpha wolf waiting for the beta to lie down and offer his belly.

I look down at the ground instead—close to the same thing, I guess. "I'm sorry. I didn't mean to... eavesdrop."

"What did you hear?" he asks.

"N-nothing. I-I swear. Nothing." I chance a glance up at him. "Are you upset with me?"

My real question is... are you going to stop teaching me in the private studio? But I don't ask it.

He smiles kindly and shakes his head, causing me to release a slow breath.

"No, Cassia. It's my fault. I shouldn't have left the door open. He'd just arrived, and I got distracted. Don't worry. Everything is fine. No harm done."

I quickly nod and excuse myself before he has a chance to change his mind.

7

It's Wednesday. Two weeks have passed since the thing happened in the shower. At our last meeting, nothing happened. Nothing sexual at least. I danced. We danced together. I showered. Alone. Is he upset with me? Has he lost interest? Did something happen in the shower that night that made him not want me? Did he decide I wasn't something he wanted after all? Is he angry? Is he punishing me for almost catching him in Mr. V.'s office?

I've spent the past week obsessing about this like some pathetic lovesick teenager. *Why doesn't he want me? Why hasn't he called me?* That's basically the thought train that runs through my head even though I know he would never call me. It would leave a record. Evidence. A thin string tying the two of us together—not that I would ever pull the string. I can't. It's mutually assured destruction.

Suddenly his whispered *soon* seems farther and farther away—a broken promise lying in shards between us. I have masturbated like a sex addict since that night together in the shower, thinking of him each time. Each time my fantasy gets dirtier, darker, so disturbing I wish I could make it stop. But the more completely he owns and controls me in the fantasy, the stronger my orgasm, the louder my moan, which bounces off the walls of my bedroom. There's no one there to hear it, but he told me to make these sounds. So I do. And somehow it seems to make the pleasure stronger when I don't hold them back—like a small reward for my obedience.

He didn't even ask at our last meeting if I followed this order. And yet still, I follow it as though there is no expiration date on his demand on my body.

I made several mistakes the last few performances. I can't believe how upset I am about him *not* touching me last week. I'm way off my game. If it gets any worse, the director could notice. I could be out of a job.

I've been in a fog. Henry and Melinda have noticed, but it's not like I can talk to them about this. How the hell would I explain it?

Does he want me to beg for it? Does he want me to shamelessly kneel and beg for him to come to the stage and fuck me? Is that what this is? I'm afraid to do that. What if he still rejects me? And why do I care? How have I allowed myself to become so wrapped up in this man? Have I forgotten why he's doing this?

I've had dinner and my bath in the warm vanilla bath oil. I'm dressed for him, and my hair is in a bun. I've just finished buttoning up a pair of jeans over my leotard when the doorbell rings. It's a few minutes after eight.

I look through the peephole, and terror grips me. There's a police officer standing on the other side. I take a slow, deep breath. I knew this would happen eventually. Someone would notice Conall was missing. Questions would be asked. Should I have reported him missing?

I should have reported him missing. I should have gone in there and cried at the police station. Or maybe that would be bad. It would call too much attention. For fuck's sake, you can't get away with murder when you're the wife. You have a link to the person. Of course they're going to question you. It's always the wife or husband. The boyfriend or girlfriend. Almost always.

The enormity of my crime hits me all at once. This strange way I've been living life like a normal girl—not a killer—is shattered in an instant.

I open the door, my face a mask of calm. "Can I help you?"

"Mrs. Walsh?"

"Yes?" I don't bother to tell him I kept my name when I married. In some weird way I think it makes me look even more suspicious—like I was never that emotionally attached to him, so of course I must be guilty.

"I'm Officer Jenkins. Do you know where your husband is?"

I mentally count back the amount of time it's been since I killed Conall. I think four or five weeks now. Shit that's a lot.

"He's supposed to be away on business," I say, hoping like hell they don't know when he was supposed to have left. He's gone away for weeks at a time before, so this isn't that unusual, but it's edging into that territory where it would look strange to anyone.

"Someone reported him missing today."

I start to cry. I can't stop the tears. Did my blackmailer give them a tip? Why? Why would he do that? I'm doing everything he wants. Even if he's lost interest in me, he told me if I obeyed him... until he was done... he wouldn't report me. He promised he'd let me go.

"Ma'am?" the officer says.

There's this part of me that knows I should ask for a lawyer, but I can't ask for a lawyer because it will just make me look guilty of something. Why would I need a lawyer in this situation if I haven't done anything wrong?

"H-he and I had a fight before he left. W-we talked about splitting up," I lie. "I wasn't sure if he was coming back. He talked like he might find an apartment or something. I've been mad at him, and things have been so crazy at the company with the dance season starting. I-is... do you think he's okay?"

This better be an Oscar-winning performance, or my life is over. Or maybe the stereotype of the weak, fragile ballerina will save me. Maybe I'm not even on their radar.

"We don't know, ma'am. Is there a good number I can reach you at? We'll let you know when we learn more."

I give him the number, and he leaves. I watch the police car pull away, then I shut the door and slide to the floor, the tears continuing to fall.

It's nine fifteen when I get to the opera house. I'm still crying, still shaken over the visit from the police.

"Did you do this?" I shout into the seemingly empty theater.

"Did I do what?" the voice fills the space. He sounds irritated at having an accusation aimed at him—as if he's an innocent. Even so, his voice is comforting at the same time it's upsetting—especially in light of the police showing up at my door.

"Did you tip them off? Did you report Conall missing?"

"No. Tell me what happened," he demands.

His voice is so sharp and urgent that it actually stops my crying. I go up onto the stage, wipe the tears off my face, and set my ballet bag down. I change out of my street shoes and into my soft canvas ballet shoes and finish getting ready while I tell him everything that happened.

I finish with, "They're going to find out. I'm going to go to prison."

"No. You will not." He says it with such certainty that I almost believe him.

"I didn't report him missing. It looks suspicious."

"You covered well," he says. "Don't worry. I'll handle it."

"What do you mean, you'll handle it?" How can he *handle* it?

"I asked you if you knew how much power I had. Conall had good money. I have *god* money. I will handle it. They will be moved off your trail. Trust me. You do not have to worry about this. The *only* person with the power to put you in prison is me. And I refuse to relinquish that power to whatever jackass reported your husband missing."

By this time, I'm standing at the barre, going through my warm-ups, trying to calm my anxiety and the trembling in my limbs that doesn't want to go away.

"Did you cancel your waxing appointment? That was today, right?" he asks, changing the subject as if this issue with the police truly is nothing.

"No, I didn't cancel. But I didn't go. I was distracted and forgot."

"Yes, you've been distracted all week. What was going on at your performances? I counted thirty-two mistakes spread across four shows. What am I going to do with you?"

I swallow hard. "P-punish me?"

"Yes."

I take a long, slow breath. My body immediately wakes up at this possibility. Should I be scared? Should I be aroused? I don't know what to feel, but he's going to touch me. Beyond the *pas de deux*. Something profoundly personal is about to happen here. And I don't have the luxury of pretending he's some secret lover and not my blackmailer, not after the words that just passed between us. And yet, still I want him.

But first he wants to see the new solo I've been working on with Mr. V. It's another one of Odette's solos from Swan Lake. He gives me some corrections, sounding irritated, losing patience with me, and I'm crying the next time I run through the solo.

He turns off the music mid-stream. "Enough," he growls. "What in the fuck is wrong with you?"

He doesn't shout at me, but this level of displeasure from him aimed in my direction makes me flinch.

"Do you or do you not want to be a principal dancer?"

"Yes, Sir. I do."

"Tell me what's going on with you. You're dancing like someone else. You're dancing like someone who is never getting out of the corps. Why?"

I shield my eyes against the spotlight on me and stare out into the vast darkness. I shake my head.

"Tell me!" he demands. "Why are you so distracted?"

I shake my head again.

"Are you still afraid of the police? I've told you I'll handle it."

"No, Sir." I am, but that's not why I'm tripping over my feet like some gangly teen. Finally I tell him. The words just spill out of me. "You didn't touch me last week."

"Of course I touched you. We danced." There's a silence, and even though I can't see him, I imagine I can. And in my mind's eye, I see the light bulb go on over his head.

"Oh," he says. It's the most smug, self-satisfied *Oh* I've ever heard spoken aloud. A moment later he says, "Put on the blindfold."

My body responds to this immediately. The words *put on the blindfold* create a pulsing throb between my legs, and I'm sure this will be my new normal. It's a trigger, a prompt. Those four words slip inside me, make me wet like some kind of arousal drug.

I hope he doesn't expect me to do the new *pas de deux* with him, because I know I won't be able to focus on it. I put on the blindfold and stand at the barre, one hand braced against it as if I need it for balance just to stand. And I wait.

A few minutes pass, and he is there, standing behind me, his chest pressed against my back, his hand resting on my hand on the barre. He leans in close to my ear.

"You're going to be punished, and you're going to be waxed. And then you will dance the *pas de deux* with me without a single misstep. Do you understand, Ms. Lane?"

"Y-yes, Sir," I gasp.

"Thirty-two errors," he growls. "It's unacceptable. You're better than that."

I need him to touch me. If he touches me, I can meet his demands for perfection. I can handle the pressure. What I can't handle is the thought that he might grow bored with me before I can prove I'm not a waste of his time.

Suddenly, his hands are in my hair, taking down the bun I so carefully put up. He runs his fingers through the long chestnut strands, letting my hair fall in loose waves around my shoulders. He pulls off my leg warmers and the soft canvas shoes.

I stand completely still as he slides the straps of my leotard down my arms. He takes the tights as well as he rolls the fabric down and off my body. When I'm naked, his hands reach around to cup my breasts. He tweaks my nipples, hard.

"Ow!" I cry out. But even though he just delivered pain, I'm even more aroused than before.

"Shhh," he says. "You have to be punished."

I wonder if that counted as punishment for one of my errors. Are there now only thirty-one small agonies left before he moves on to the next thing on his sadistic to-do list? What is wrong with me that I crave any touch from him?

He takes my hand and guides me away from the barre. "Kneel and spread your legs. Forehead on the floor. Arms stretched out in front of you." He helps and guides me into the position he wants me in.

"Stay," he says.

I take a deep breath as he walks away. I've spent the last week obsessing about him, fantasizing about him, wanting him to touch me. But now, the reality of my situation crashes into me hard. And I'm suddenly reminded just how fucked-up this is. He's going to hurt me. Conall hurt me. I thought this man was in control, but now I'm not so sure. If he isn't, what does that mean for me? And suddenly I'm crying again.

He returns, and I hear something heavy being set down on the ground near me. Then he sits next to me and strokes my back and that sweet spot on my neck, the same way he touched me in the shower two weeks ago.

"Shhh, you're safe," he says. Which is so completely ridiculous. I am not safe. The police are asking questions. I'm kneeling naked on the stage of an abandoned opera house waiting to be *punished* for minor dance mistakes by a man I don't know. This is as far as I can possibly get from safe. But if the words *put the blindfold on* make me aroused, *Shhh you're safe* makes my entire body relax and press against his hand for more comfort.

Sensual piano music begins to play over the sound system. He lays something on the ground next to my hand.

"Explore it with your fingers," he says.

This isn't a sexual command, but I swear everything he says now sounds like the dirtiest thing any human being has ever uttered. I move my fingers over long strands of leather, interspersed with ribbons. Both the ribbons and leather end in knots.

"It's a flogger," he says.

He takes it away, and then I feel him standing behind me. I tense.

"Relax," he says. "Just surrender to this."

Why haven't I tried to fight him? Is this threat of blackmail really so powerful that I wouldn't fight at all? That I would barely plead? I haven't even done that tonight. I can't bring myself to.

I feel guilty for the thirty-two errors, even though they don't personally affect him. They displease him. I want to erase them. I want to be perfect.

I cringe at this thought, reminded of the movie I watched with Henry and Melinda. Suddenly I'm that neurotic girl on the screen. What would my friends think if they could see me now?

Drink. And then they'd toss back a shot in my honor.

I'm jolted out of my thoughts as he drags the flogger across my back. A tickling whisper of touch. This feels sexual. Intimate. And I realize I would rather he do this than not touch me beyond dancing.

The way he dances with me is intimate, but it's not enough. It's only a tease. Suddenly, I wonder about the women who have danced with him. Did he take them as lovers? I think it would be cruel to them if he didn't.

The flogger strikes in a stinging kiss across my back.

"Count," he says.

"One."

It hurts, but in a way I want to move closer to. It's complex, like a finely aged wine. There are layers and notes. Flavors. Like peach and vanilla if peach and vanilla were tactile sensations instead of tastes.

He falls into a rhythm with the flogger, and I fall into one with my answering count. I assume there will be thirty-two. It isn't painful enough for that to seem like torture. Each strike, followed by a number, followed by an echoing throb from my pussy. The longer this goes on, the more excited I get, the more desperately I need him to rut into me like an animal in the middle of the stage floor. All I can think about is that long, thick, hard cock pounding inside me in yet another dark rhythm.

When will he fuck me? When?

"Count!" he says.

"Twenty-seven," I say. Five more.

Except that the flogger doesn't fall against my flesh again. Instead, he walks a few steps away. I hear some things moved about, and it finally occurs to my addled brain that the heavy thing he set down was some sort of box that he's searching through.

He returns and lays something else beside me.

"Touch it," he says.

Again, my mind goes to a dirty place even though I know he means for me to touch whatever he took from the box. It is long and thin, hard.

"It's a cane," he says, as if I would never have divined this on my own.

I understand on a certain level that this man could make any implement hurt if he put enough of his power behind it. Likewise, he can use each implement in a gentle way—in a caress—no matter what that implement is. But a cane is... serious. A cane is meant to hurt. In countries that use these in punishment for crimes, it often scars people for life.

Tears that didn't trouble me during the last few minutes, stream down my face in fear and anticipation of this abrupt escalation in my punishment. He pries the cane from my questing fingers and presses it lightly against the top of my head which still rests on the floor.

"Raise your head and kiss it," he says.

I do this, my lips pressing reverently against the bamboo as if this act can appease him, as if this obedience will make him say the magic words, *I think that's enough for tonight*—words I didn't want to hear two weeks ago, but desperately want to hear now.

"Please," I whimper.

"Thirty-two errors, Cassia," he says as if this explains everything about why we're here. "You will count. Start at twenty-eight."

I feel the brush of air as he moves behind me.

A moment later, the cane slices through the air to land against my ass. I cry out.

"Count," he demands.

But the breath has left me for a moment. "T-twenty-eight," I manage when I catch my breath again.

"Good girl."

This praise irrationally pleases me. I should be angry. What is this man doing to my suddenly fragile mind?

Before I can think about that, the cane falls again, just below the first strike. I shriek. I know he's holding back. He's not trying to actually harm me, but still it's an intense screaming sort of pain. "Twenty-nine," I say, tears coming faster.

After the next one, I beg him to stop. But he is implacable.

"Two more."

I count the thirty-first and beg again. "Please... please... I can't take anymore... please..." I'm sobbing now. Even though I know it's just one more, one more is still too many and seems impossible.

The cane falls again, this final sting feeling as though it grips me and shakes me and breaks me apart.

"T-thirty-two," I gasp out.

"Good girl." He sits beside me, pulls me into his arms, holds me, strokes my hair and my back, runs his fingertips lightly over the welts he left, and just lets me cry it out. A hand slips between my legs, his finger pressing into me.

"You are so fucking wet. So perfect," he growls against my ear.

I cling to him, my hips moving in answer to his exploring fingers. He presses his lips to my forehead, then tilts my chin up, claiming my mouth in a searing kiss.

Yes, my mind sighs.

"Are you all right?" he asks.

"Yes, Sir." And I am. The cane hurt. It was intense, but I know he hasn't damaged me. And he wasn't angry. This wasn't anger. This was controlled. I can feel his erection through his pants. What just happened was as stimulating to him as it was to me.

He stands with me in his arms and carries me a few feet,

then he gently lays me down on the dance tarp. The vinyl material is cool against my warm back and ass.

He leaves me for a moment. I'm dimly aware that the piano music is still playing. He returns and spreads my legs wide. I feel my face flame, knowing he will get a close-up visual of just how aroused I am. But he makes no comment about this.

He just quietly waxes me. I've had this done so many times that I just lie there, soaking up the warmth of the wax. I'm so used to waxing that the pain of it doesn't bother me. It's kind of soothing in a strange way. It's usually a huge endorphin rush, though I can already feel the endorphins flooding me from the flogger and the cane.

If he had started by waxing me, I would probably be more self-conscious, but after what just happened, something has shifted deep within me. I'm so completely his in this moment that although vulnerable and exposed to him, I don't feel what I expected to feel. It's as though my body truly is his, to punish, to pleasure, to groom in whatever way pleases him.

When he's finished, he cleans me off with a wet rag. It's cool. I have no idea where he got the water—maybe one of the water bottles that seem to appear by magic. I hear a jar open and smell the distinct scent of coconut oil. He massages the oil into my freshly waxed skin.

There is no possible way I can dance after this. I'll only mess up. I'll only earn more punishment. I'm about to say this, to beg for whatever small amount of mercy this man may have. But before I can give voice to these thoughts, he lifts me up and carries me to the table. He sits me in the chair and gives me water. Then he hand feeds me a ham and cheese sandwich. I'm not hungry, but I'm grateful for the food. It helps me return to myself after such an intense experience.

"Stay," he commands.

I sit in this darkness behind the blindfold, waiting, straining to hear whatever he's doing. I do hear things, like something being dragged across the floor. Something soft and thuddy more than hard and scrapey. But I have no idea what it is. I'm so tired. I just want to rest.

He returns to me, picks me up, and carries me a few feet. He lays me down gently on a mattress with soft silky sheets and a pillow my head sinks into. He covers my naked body with a blanket and presses a kiss to my forehead.

"Wait ten seconds, then remove the blindfold. I want you to rest for a bit. If you fall asleep, I'll wake you when I'm ready."

His weight lifts off the mattress, and I feel more than hear him recede into the distance. I take a deep breath and count to ten. When I remove the blindfold, I'm alone on the stage. I sit up and blink slowly. He's dimmed the spotlight so the light I'm exposed to now isn't overpowering, but is instead soft.

I lie back down and close my eyes and rest.

I don't know how much time has passed when he wakes me. I don't know what time it was when I lay down. I'm gently roused from sleep with warm lips pressed against mine, a strong hand stroking my breast.

"Wake up, and dance the *pas de deux* with me."

I feel rested and refreshed, as though he timed my nap just right so he would wake me just after a REM cycle. I don't feel groggy. I do feel a little sore and achy from the cane and from the waxing. But otherwise, I feel kind of amazing like I spent a full day at the spa.

I realize the blindfold is covering my eyes again. He helps me sit up and just holds me for a few minutes.

"Are you ready to dance? It's almost midnight. We'll do the *pas de deux* once, and then I'll let you go."

A very strange Cinderella story, I decide.

Once I'm awake, he helps me into my *pointe* shoes and then pulls me up to stand. I'm still naked except for the shoes. This feels so strange, so exposed—even after all that has happened tonight.

"Stay," he says softly.

The mattress is dragged away. He guides me to the middle of the stage—or what I assume must be the middle. The music starts.

We dance together so perfectly that I'm sure I must really still be asleep. This must be a dream. Every time we dance together, I trust his holds and lifts more and more. I know he won't drop me. He won't let me fall. If I stumble, he'll catch me.

The song ends.

"Good girl. Do well at this week's performances, and next week I'll reward you. All pleasure. Would you like that?"

"Yes, Sir," I whimper. I want to stop there. I really do. I try so hard to stop there, but I can't. "Please Sir... please fuck me." The shameful words tumble out of my mouth beyond my control.

"I'm sorry, no. Next week."

"You don't have to let me come. Use me. Take your pleasure. Please I need..." I clamp my mouth down hard. I swear I will bite my own tongue to shut myself up if I have to. I can't believe that many appalling words slipped out before I could stop them.

He chuckles. He has me. He knows just how far I've fallen into his snare. It amuses him that I would trade my pleasure away just to feel his cock inside me.

"Next week, cupcake."

Warmth moves through me at the introduction of this pet

name, and it's almost enough to make up for the absence of what I need from him so badly. My mind immediately goes back to the buttercream frosting on his fingers that first night.

On any other man's lips, *cupcake* would be offensive, demeaning. But when he says it, it makes me feel cared for, like the care he took to bake for me even if it was wrapped in so many threats. It's hard to remember that last part.

He dismisses me to go shower. As the water heats and steam fills the bathroom, I stand naked in front of the mirror, avoiding my eyes, twisting my body to see the perfect row of cane welts across my ass. My fingertips graze over the indentations.

I glance up to see a second camera has been installed since the last time I was in here. It's a few feet away in a corner next to the ceiling, and I know he's watching me as I look at and touch these welts. I wonder if I'll bruise. I wonder what it says about me that these hidden marks seem so different from the ones Conall gave me.

These are claiming marks that say I belong to this man. They are proof that we are two real people doing this twisted thing together. They make our secret real.

8

J ust as he said, the police don't bother me again. On
Friday, a few hours before the show, and around
closing time for most normal jobs, I get a phone call.
It's the police chief. It seems very unusual that the
police chief would call me.

My heart hammers wildly as I listen to what he has to say.
He tells me that he's very sorry I was bothered the other day by
one of his officers. The guy was new and overstepped his
duties. The police chief tells me he understands Conall and I
had a complicated relationship and that I may be quite
relieved if my husband never shows up again. And this is
understandable, he says.

He tells me Conall is under suspicion of being mixed up in
a lot of highly illegal activity which he is not at liberty to tell
me about, though the words *Irish Mob* get thrown out in passing. They suspect he fled the country under a new name and
could be anywhere by now.

The chief says he would be very surprised if he ever
returns to this city or even the country. Then he goes on about

protocols for how long it will be before they can legally declare Conall dead—for my sake—so that the house becomes fully mine and the accounts become fully mine. He says the department is here for me in whatever way I need and not to hesitate to reach out if I need *anything at all.* The way he says this seems to extend truly to anything and doesn't seem to be only about this issue with *Conall fleeing the country.* The chief assures me that otherwise no one from the department will disturb me again.

It's a surreal phone call. *Very* surreal. I thank the chief, disconnect the call, and just stare at the phone in my hand as if it might transform into a snake and strike. What in the actual fuck just happened?

I mean I don't know all that much about police procedure. What I do know, I've learned from television shows, which I'm told aren't very accurate. But I know what just happened isn't normal. That officer that came to my house didn't *overstep his duties.* He was just doing his job as officially laid out.

My blackmailer's boasts of his own power being far greater than Conall's, of his wealth dwarfing Conall's, were not empty. I know with every fiber of my being that he did this. Somehow. I don't know how. Is the department dirty? Did he pay the chief off with some ridiculous sum to free me? A freedom I'm well aware he can take back at any time.

Or maybe Conall *was* mixed up in something. I'm really not entirely clear about things. He owned several businesses: a chain of hardware stores, some restaurants and Irish pubs, a few night clubs. But I don't know much about it or which establishments he specifically owned. I know he went to work in an office building somewhere in the city where he presumably did office-type work managing his businesses. I know his secretary was the Delectable Stella. Is that weird? Or is it normal? That he had all these businesses and had some official office building set up? I don't know.

The more I think about this, the weirder I think it is that I knew so little real information about Conall's life outside of me. It seems suspicious, like he must have been doing something very wrong to keep me so hermetically sealed off from his life.

Everything between us always seemed to revolve around his jealousy and irritation over whatever minor thing he'd decided was a major catastrophe in our relationship at the moment. It was all about fear of what he would do to me and how I knew I could never escape him.

I can't escape my blackmailer either. But somehow even though I should—especially after the cane—I don't feel that same threat with him. I want to run to him, not away from him. Even if I have to run blindfolded. It's only been two days since I was with him. The welts and soreness remain with me, as though his hands have stayed on me even in his absence.

Was Conall in the Irish Mob? I think it must be some crafted story to put all the pieces in neat ordered rows, to close this chapter of my life once and for all with no loose ends, but I don't know. You hear a lot about the Italian Mob. You even hear about the Russian Mob. But you never fucking hear about the Irish. Most normal people forget there even IS an Irish Mob. Or they think there was one, early in the 19th century, maybe early in the 20th as well, but that somehow they just faded into the mists of time or returned to the rolling green landscape of Ireland as if whisked away there by fairies.

But they are out there. And Conall could have been one of them. I have no idea. But what I do know is... this was *handled* for me. Just like I was told it would be.

This should make me more afraid. Someone even more

dangerous and powerful, someone with no face and no name... has this absolute power over me. *I* should change my name and flee the country—if I even knew how to do that. But then I couldn't dance. And all I've ever wanted was to dance. And just fuck it all if I can't do that one fucking thing.

I'm only free if I'm on a stage. In prison or a fugitive is all the same to me. And so I belong to this man who holds my life in his hands, who just pulled strings to free me from the consequences of murder, who claims he plans to elevate me in the company if I prove to him I can be a principal. There's no longer any doubt that whatever this man wants, he will get, whether from me or anyone else in his path. Even so, the doubt lingers that he can or will make me a principal.

I don't know why I hang onto this doubt. I guess it's because it's all I've ever wanted, and if I believe it will happen and it doesn't, I don't think I'll recover. I can't allow myself to hope. Even if he can do it, maybe he just wants to dangle it in front of me like a carrot. I can understand why he handled the police. If the police got suspicious and took me in for questioning, my blackmailer loses control of the narrative, and it's obvious that the only currency he truly wants to possess is power. Control. He feeds on it and on me like a vampire with blood.

I spend the next ten minutes or so as I get ready to go to the theater fighting with myself over whether or not I should think of this man as my blackmailer. I mean he *is* my blackmailer. But when I think of a blackmailer, I think of someone who demands small unmarked bills in a paper bag left under a park bench every Thursday afternoon at two p.m. Not... this.

I want to call him my lover, but we aren't exactly having sex, and is he my lover if it's coerced? Is it coerced? I can't pretend I haven't desperately wanted every single touch from him. Even the punishment.

I can't pretend it hasn't all excited me, but does my wanting him even matter? What if I didn't? What would he do then? I can't bring myself to test this theory because I don't want him to stop. So it just rattles around in my brain, haunting and tormenting me.

Three hours later when the curtain goes up and I'm on stage, he's in the box seat. I see his shadow outlined there. I feel his eyes on me. I let out a relieved breath and feel unreasonably safe, protected in this moment. Even though I realize exactly how crazy this thought is.

I dance better than I've danced since all this started because for the first time, I have the smallest hope that even if I can never be truly free, he will at least let me dance. And that's free enough.

9

I t's Monday morning. The entire company is in Studio A. Every single dancer. Every single choreographer, instructor, the director, the ballet master. Everyone. Something big is about to happen. We can all feel it, but we all pretend we don't, running through our warm-ups and stretches at the barre as a sense of nervousness moves through the room like an electric current.

So far, the men and women running the company have been off in a corner of the studio having a private discussion, so technically, they haven't really "entered the studio" in terms of etiquette because they are collected in their own group full of low whispers and nods. Finally, they break from this cluster and come over to where we are. All the dancers stop what they're doing and turn to greet them. The dancers who were stretching on the floor stand.

"Good morning, company," Mr. V. says.

"Good morning, Mr. V.," the company answers back.

"I have some exciting news. We'll of course be doing our annual two week run of The Nutcracker in December."

This isn't his big news. This is just the introduction.

A barely audible sense of grumbling ripples through the room. We all fucking hate The Nutcracker. And we hate it because it's the only ballet most people know anything about. And we have to perform it every single year with no deviations. It doesn't rotate in and out like many other repertoire ballets. It's just always there. I don't know a single professional dancer who feels giddy about The Nutcracker.

Mr. V. ignores the response, largely because it's an involuntary reaction for the most part, and it happens every year. Then he continues.

"However, in a few weeks, we'll start working on Firebird. We have a guest choreographer coming in with exciting new choreography I know everyone will love. The full cast list is posted beside my office door. But I would like to take a moment to announce a promotion and welcome our new principal dancer, Cassia Lane."

There's a ringing in my ears as I try to determine if he really just said my name or if I got lost in a fantasy again. But Mr. V. is looking right at me and smiling warmly. "Cassia will be our firebird this season."

I know my mystery blackmailer said he could elevate me. I wanted to believe it, but deep down I didn't. Now I do. The depth of his silent power here is astounding.

I could tell myself Mr. V. just *saw something in me* and made the decision in concert with the others at the head of the company, but Conall was paying to keep me in the corps. That means his donation was at least matched to get me here, otherwise my talent could never overcome the economics of the situation.

"I've been working privately with Cassia to get her up to speed with the rest of the principals," Mr. V. adds. In this single statement, he's just saved my reputation—offering a neat explanation for his Monday afternoons with me in the small private studio. He's saved me from being viewed as some whore who let him between my legs for a promotion, not that anyone in the company doubts my legitimate talent.

Everyone is stunned. I hear whispers from some of the principals. The only clear sentence I can pick out among the murmurs is: "That role should be Natalie's."

I glance over to Natalie. She looks shocked as well. I know she wanted this role. I know she expected to have this role. Only moments ago, when the new Firebird was announced, she was no doubt excited, imagining herself soaring through the air in a fiery red costume. And I can't blame her for that.

This woman has the power to ruin my life at the company. She has the power to make every day a living hell for me. She's a senior principal and the top prima ballerina here, and by right, all the best roles are hers. Every dancer here defers to her. They respect her.

Natalie moves from her place at the barre with the other principals and crosses the studio to me with purpose. There is absolute pin-drop silence. I can almost hear the sound of a slap across my face. But the expected retribution doesn't happen.

Instead, she smiles and hugs me and whispers in my ear. "You will make a beautiful firebird. You deserve this. I'm so happy for you."

This is a severe break in ballet etiquette, but no one chastises her because every single person in this studio from the ballet master down to the newest member of the corps knows that this is important. If Natalie accepts me, they all accept me.

She takes my hand and guides me over to the set of barres where the principals stand, and room is made for me. Then everyone in the studio, previously frozen by this news and Natalie's actions, breaks out into applause. Mr. V. nods his approval at Natalie as if he had no doubt she would be classy about this.

Rehearsal starts as though nothing monumental and world changing just happened to me.

When we break for lunch, Natalie guides me back to the special set of dressing rooms reserved for the principals. There's a large dressing room for the men and one for the women. Each dancer has a generous specific space to get ready in. In the middle, connecting the two dressing rooms, is a large lounge. It's reminiscent of a school teacher's lounge in a way or an office break room.

There are tables and a refrigerator and microwave, a counter and a sink. There are a few couches and a large flat screen TV on the wall and a video game console. The other walls are covered in dance posters. I've never seen the inside of this room. It's a perk for the principals.

Natalie shows me to a place of my very own in the women's side of the dressing rooms, and then she takes me out into the hallway to a private space to talk. My heart is in my throat. Is this when the mask slips? Is she going to let the claws out now? Is she going to beat the crap out of me so I can't dance and take this role from her?

Before she can speak, I say, "Natalie, I'm so sorry... I didn't know they would... I had no idea about any of this... that part should be yours." And it should be.

But she's still smiling—not a fake smile. "Cassia, relax. I'm not mad. You really do deserve this. It hasn't been announced yet, but I'm leaving at the end of the season and moving to another company."

"But why...?" Maybe she got a better offer. And it's not my

business anyway. Natalie Dumas is a fixture here. It seems impossible that she could ever leave.

She shrugs and laughs. "I'm in love. He's a principal at the company I'm joining. Long distance was getting too hard for us. There was finally an opening, and I auditioned a few weeks ago. So yes, I would love to be the firebird—especially with new choreography. But my future isn't here. And yours is."

"Do the others know yet?"

She shakes her head. "No, I just found out recently. I told the director before the performance last Thursday, and he asked me not to say anything until today. Listen, when I'm gone, you're going to be the queen bee around here."

I balk at that. That's ridiculous. "But I only just got promoted..."

She shakes her head. "You know that's not how this hierarchy works. You're my replacement. They want you at the top of the company. If they didn't, they wouldn't make you the firebird in the middle of the season. They're making a definite statement with this choice. They didn't tell me this ahead of time, but trust me on this one. You're their new star. So when I leave, I need you to keep the group together. Don't let it devolve into nasty cattiness. This company works better when we all support each other."

It's a myth that all dancers are vicious competitive assholes to each other. At the same time, people are human, and at some companies, dancers *are* vicious competitive assholes to each other. But not here, and the reason for that is Natalie.

She continues. "Don't abuse your power. Don't be cruel to any of the dancers. Don't call them out in front of others if you don't absolutely have to."

"I won't. I would never..."

She nods. "Let's go to the lounge. I need to let the others

know I'm leaving. They don't need to hear it from somewhere else and think it's because of you."

Frederick, the top male principal who normally dances with Natalie, comes over to us when we enter the lounge. I stare at him for a long moment. I know he can't be my tormentor, the man in the private box, because he was on stage dancing during that time.

But I also don't know for sure that my blackmailer actually *is* the man in the box. That could all just be a fantasy in my head... a story I'm telling myself. But whoever is behind my turn in fate had the money to make up for the lost money from Conall. Even a top principal dancer doesn't make the kind of money to match Conall's contribution. But I don't know Frederick's personal finances. He could be independently wealthy. And I've never really talked to him.

My blackmailer is obviously both a dancer and somebody who knows the Swan Lake choreography. Oh, fuck, what if I'm wrong about the private box? Is Frederick the man I've been meeting and *doing things with* on the stage of the old opera house every Wednesday? Is this the man I call Sir?

I can't stop the blush at this thought. I want to sink into the floor and disappear.

"Welcome to the top of the food chain, Cassia," he says with a wink.

I let out a breath. No. This is not my mystery lover. His voice is different. I smile weakly back at him.

"I'll be dancing the firebird with you," he says.

I glance over to Natalie, who gives me an *I told you so* look. She's right. The company is sending a clear signal. They absolutely would not pair me with Frederick in the middle of the season like this if I weren't Natalie's replacement.

The other principals are in the lounge by now. They watch

me with a certain wariness. They saw Natalie's reaction, so they aren't ready to lynch me just yet, but should they get the signal, they will pounce on me like ravening hyenas.

Natalie tells them what she just told me out in the hallway. It gets very emotional. There's crying. Even a few of the male principals tear up. The depth of love they have for this woman eclipses even what I thought I knew. She promises she's just a plane ride away, and she'll visit.

Frederick looks not less sad, but less shocked than the others. He must have known about the boyfriend at the other company and seen this coming.

We all go out together for lunch at a local restaurant. I make it a point to speak individually to each of the male principals, but none of them is *him*. The man who owns my life is not one of the men at this table.

When I get back, Melinda and Henry practically maul me.

"I told you!" Henry says, sweeping me up like only a long-time dance partner can manage. "I knew you were the best dancer here!"

And now I'm sad, because although I'm excited to be dancing with Frederick, this means I won't be dancing with Henry any longer. He senses the sadness, and I know he feels it, too, but then he says, "I got paired with Melinda for this one. It's all good, don't worry. I will survive."

"This is so exciting!" Melinda squeals. Of course she wishes it were her. There is no corps dancer who doesn't fantasize about the magical moment I had this morning. But she's happy for me, and her hug and congratulations are genuine.

I'm glad at least she gets to dance with Henry. It feels less like we're all being split up.

10

W hen I walk down the darkened aisle in the theater of the opera house, his voice booms out over the speaker. "Congratulations, Ms. Lane, I hear you'll be replacing Natalie. And the new Firebird. I hope you won't forget the little people... like me."

Right. Like I could ever forget. Like he didn't orchestrate this. I wonder briefly if he pulled the puppet strings behind Natalie's departure as well. Did he know about the boyfriend? It feels like he knows everything about everything, at least at the company. Did he nudge another dancer out and make room for her to audition so he could maneuver me into this role?

I shake the thought from my head. That truly *is* crazy. I know this guy has a lot of money and a lot of power, but he's not an *actual* god. *Get a grip, Cassia.*

"Undress," he says. "Take everything off. I want you nude except for *pointe* shoes."

Even though he's seen me naked, this request startles me and makes me self-conscious. "C-can I warm up first?"

"You can warm up in just the shoes."

"Leg warmers?" I ask. "Please... Sir... I need..."

"I will allow leg warmers, but just until you're finished with your barre."

I swallow hard. This man is both completely strange and completely familiar to me. There's a certain shyness I'm sure I can never overcome until and unless I'm allowed to see this man's face.

I fear I'll never see it. He's a disembodied voice, hands, and cock. A swirl of demands, threats, and promises—interweaving pleasure and pain.

Dark strains of cello music play over the sound system as I take off my clothes. I sit nude on the ground and put my *pointe* shoes on. I slip the pink leg warmers over them, then rise with all the poise and grace trained into me for two decades, and go to the barre.

I wonder how far away he is. At what angle does he view me? Is there any possible angle of nude *pliés* that isn't grotesquely lewd? I push past these thoughts and complete the exercises. I wonder if he's stroking himself as he watches this. The idea excites me even as I know it should repulse me.

The music fades, and he speaks, interrupting my warm ups. "Cassia, have you ever paused to consider that I might not be your only audience? The theater is dark. The spotlight is bright. It would be quite impossible to know, not only where I am, but if I have friends."

I freeze. I'm horrified by this idea. Embarrassed. Scared. I want to grab my things and run, but if there are others, what might they do? Could he stop them? Would he bother?

But behind the sharp tang of fear—this almost overwhelming sensation of anxiety and panic—is that old familiar throbbing pulse between my legs as my body grows wet at this idea, practically eager for an audience to voyeuristically observe my fall to this dark and powerful man. Some twisted part of me wants an audience. Maybe it's an occupational hazard.

"You aren't finished warming up, Ms. Lane. Continue," he says.

I consider my options and realize I have no options. Of course no one else is here. I know that. Intellectually I know that. It would be far too risky to bring others into this. But you can't tell this to my emotions. You can't tell this to my fear.

I imagine who he could have out in the audience. Other powerful people, no doubt? Or people from the company? Male Principals? Mr. V.? No, Mr. V. could never behave in the professional way he does with me if he were privy to what happens on this stage. I feel the blush creep up my neck as I consider this.

I marvel at my ability not to cry, scream, beg. Not to flee from the stage. To simply stand at the barre and obey. I'm an utter professional.

When I've completed my warm-ups, he says, "Good girl. Put the blindfold on."

The trigger.

I put the blindfold on and wait, my body surging with anticipation, wetness flooding me, preparing me for whatever he might choose to penetrate me with. Fingers, toy, cock, tongue? I'm ready for any and all of it as my ears strain to hear his approach.

As always, I feel him before I hear him—this almost extrasensory perception I have where this man is concerned.

"You did very well this week. Not only was I impressed with your performance the last time we danced together, but your technique at all your shows was flawless. I spoke with the decision makers after Friday night's performance. I paid the necessary money to free them from Conall's demands."

"Were they worried about upsetting him?" Most people seemed to worry about upsetting my husband. I wonder if they had reservations even with the extra money to supposedly *free them*.

"I let them in on the gossip about your husband."

"Gossip?" I ask.

"Irish Mob. Fled the country," he confirms. "They were very excited to be able to promote you. V. was especially pleased."

"Thank you, Sir," I say. Because gratitude seems appropriate in this moment. I knew he made this happen, and so I can't not thank him. He just changed my life completely. He just made me the star of the company, a dream I thought would never materialize into solid reality.

All the roles I thought I'd never dance suddenly stretch out before me. Mine to claim. I could have a long, bright future ahead.

I flinch when his hand presses against my cheek.

"Shhh, you're safe."

I really do feel like his well-trained dog. These commands he gives, my trained responses. How easy it is for him to calm me with a word, even in the face of this twisted arrangement between us.

He slowly strokes my cheek, and I find myself leaning into his touch.

"Does it excite you to think others might be watching? That someone might touch themselves watching me fuck you?"

"Yes, Sir," I whisper.

"Say it louder, cupcake. We want our audience to hear."

"Yes, Sir," I say louder. I still don't know if he's fucking with me. *Is* someone else in the audience? Of course not.

I may have committed a felony, but he's engaging in one as well. He can't risk anyone else knowing about this. It has to remain a secret. I tell myself this over and over, but suddenly I can feel other eyes on me. Is this my imagination? Or is it real?

I don't know the answer. The blindfold has sharply distorted my reality. Not being able to see him... to only hear him and feel him, to be this helpless and isolated, I don't know what's real.

"You dirty little slut," he says. But his voice is an approving growl. "I knew you were the perfect slut to train."

I'm not a slut. I've never been a slut. I've been shockingly chaste all things considered. I've only slept with Conall. I wasn't in a convent or anything, but with dance, I never had time for much of a social life. I could have and probably would have gotten involved with a dancer at the company eventually, but Conall was there first.

Which was my bad luck.

A year ago, when the full enormity of my situation with my husband had hit me, I'd realized with utter horror that he might be the only man I ever slept with for the rest of my life. I couldn't imagine an affair—I was too afraid. And I couldn't imagine him ever letting me go. I would never know the touch of a man who knew what to do with a woman's body.

But this man now before me, this man whose hand still hasn't left my cheek... He knows. He knows exactly what to do with a woman's body. He knows every secret desire, every fantasy, even without me giving voice to it.

His hand slides down to my throat, gripping me, but not hard. It's an assertion of dominance, of his power over me. As if I need reminders. He releases me, his hand moving down to rest on my waist.

"Open your mouth."

My mouth falls open, and his tongue sweeps inside. He could have just kissed me. I would have responded without the verbal command. But he enjoys keeping me on edge. He enjoys my obedience... all the ways he asks me to make myself vulnerable to him. All these risks he asks me to take in service of his demands.

He stops kissing me, and a moment later, his mouth is latched onto my breast, sucking my nipple into a hardened point. He steps back from me, and a whimper escapes my throat at the lost contact.

"Please..." I whisper.

"Second position. And *Relevé*."

I'm so frustrated. Last week he promised me pleasure. He promised if I was good that this week would be all about pleasure, and he's teasing me. But I do as he says. I extend my arm out to the side in a gently rounded curve, move my feet into a wider stance, and rise up onto *pointe*.

"Good girl. Under no circumstances are you to break your lines."

As if I would break my lines. I've stood up on *pointe* for ten minutes at a time to strengthen my feet. People not in the dance world mistakenly believe that the toes take all the weight, but they don't. It's the box of the shoe supporting us. A lot of it is strength, of course, but the shoes are at least half the magic.

I'm sure this will be easy. But then I shudder as his tongue sweeps over my clit. I gasp at the unexpected contact and almost falter.

He smacks my ass. "Lines!" he growls.

I hold my position as he takes his time feasting upon me. He licks, and kisses, and plunges his tongue deep inside my welcoming body. After he finishes this exploration, he returns his attention to my clit. I squeeze my eyes shut behind the blindfold, trying desperately to hold this precarious position he's put me in.

When I'm at the edge of my orgasm, he pulls away.

"No! Please... please..." It takes everything inside me not to move toward him, or at least toward where I think he is. I'm still holding my position. It feels like it's been a thousand years, but in all likelihood has been less than five minutes. I'm not tired yet, so it can't have been very long.

"When you come, I want you to be loud. I want them to be able to hear your moan all the way in the cheap seats. Do you understand, cupcake?"

"Y-yes, Sir," I manage. I'm starting to really worry someone is watching us. At the same time there is this dark and decadent place within me that thrills at this possibility even as I'm horrified by it.

His mouth is between my legs again; his tongue is forceful, demanding. He sucks on my clit. There is such a frenzy in him that it demands my body's response. I grip the barre harder, but I don't moan; I scream out my pleasure. If we aren't alone, there's no question that my voice is heard all the way back in the *cheap seats*.

His mouth latches harder on me, sucking the liquid out of me as though he's drinking me for sustenance. Finally, I'm able to quiet my cries. But he isn't done yet. He pushes his tongue inside me like a starving man licking his plate clean.

Finally he stops. Finally he's had enough. "Relax," he says.

I lower myself out of *relevé*, and bring my arm down to the side, my limbs trembling both from the effort and the force of my release.

I feel him stand up, and then he's petting my hair. "Good girl. Stretch. Loosen up. Then we'll do the *pas de deux*."

I don't know what possesses him to think I can *dance* after that. Even with as much as his tongue took, I'm still dripping wet. This sensation is made more dramatic by the bare flesh of my pussy, still fresh from where he waxed me.

"I...I need clothes," I say.

"No. You don't."

I knew before I asked that he would make me dance naked again. I stretch, and move around. I do some *pliés* and a few *rond de jambe*.

"Here. Drink." He presses a bottle of water into my hands, and I gratefully drink.

He leads me to the center of the stage, the music starts, and we dance. It's a miracle I'm able to dance, that I don't miss the steps and trip all over myself—not only because of the world-shattering orgasm I just had, but because of the worry that he wasn't kidding about an audience.

He's behind me, holding me in an embrace as the music ends. He leans close to my ear. "You become the music. It flows into you, and you flow into it. Dancers like you come along once in a lifetime."

I flush with pleasure at this compliment. It's enough to make me forget the mind-fuck of wondering if we are truly alone in this space.

He guides me back to the barre, placing one of my hands on the wood so I can steady myself.

"Kneel for me like I taught you," he says softly.

I do, and he strokes my face as he guides his cock into my mouth. I suck him sweetly and obediently. I swallow when he comes. It has become another point of etiquette between us. Just as I would never falter in calling him Sir, or obeying his commands at the barre, I would never dare refuse to swallow.

There is something deeply and seriously wrong with me. The control he takes of me in these three hours each week is absolute. But outside of this time and space, my life is more my own than it ever was with Conall. I feel freer than I've felt in years.

And I'm so grateful for everything. For Conall being gone. For the police turning their attentions away from me. For the promotion in the company. For the pleasure I just received from my captor's mouth.

He pulls out of me and pets my hair. "Such a good girl."

My face is turned up toward his waiting for more instruction.

"Are you on birth control?"

"Yes, Sir." Birth control is an absolute necessity. An unwanted pregnancy can ruin a professional dancer's life. There's the morning after pill, and abortion, but we don't fuck around when it comes to birth control.

"Good. Stay on it."

"Please..." I stop myself from begging again for him to fuck me, remembering the humiliation of the last time I asked and his rejection.

"I will fuck you when I'm ready to fuck you," he says, knowing the words I forced back down my throat even though I didn't speak them aloud this time.

I nod.

I don't know how long we've been here tonight, but he guides me to the mattress. I don't know when it got on stage, and I wonder if it was there all along and I just didn't notice it before. Or maybe... someone else... dragged it out. I push that thought away.

I feel the brightness of the spotlight on me like sunlight as he lays me down on the mattress, spreading my legs wide. He spends the next forever languidly stroking every inch of me. He plays with my pussy, making me come so many times I lose count. Just when I think I can't take anymore pleasure, he pulls another orgasm from me along with my desperate whimpers and grateful moans.

He removes my *pointe* shoes and then carefully massages all the tightness and tension out of each foot. I can't decide which is better, this gentle, yet firm way he's touching my feet, or the orgasms. I sigh in contentment.

He rolls me onto my stomach.

"Stay," he commands.

I stay. I always stay. I'm so addicted to this stranger that it doesn't even occur to me to beg or run. My will is bound to him more tightly than if he'd used actual restraints.

He returns and sits beside me on the mattress. My cheek is pressed into the soft silk of the pillow. I'm so sated. He does that wonderful rubbing at the back of my neck, causing my body to loosen even more. His fingertips trail up and down my back and over the curve of my hip.

A moment later, a cold, wet piece of metal presses between my cheeks. I gasp and stiffen at the invasion.

"Relax, and let me inside your ass."

The way he talks to me... something in his voice makes my body helplessly open to him. It makes me long to fulfill every desire and demand. The only thing I want is to please him.

I breathe slowly in and out in rhythm to the agonizingly slow way he penetrates me with this toy.

"Don't worry. I'll fuck you long before I claim your ass," he says.

I want to ask: What is this thing between us? Does it mean anything to him? Does he think of me like I think of him? Does he long for me like I long for him? Or is this all just a game of power and control? Is this some private inside joke for him to enjoy at my expense?

Finally he stops. A mewl of protest leaves my mouth as he takes the toy away. Moments later, I feel cold metal around my throat.

"I'm ready for you to call me Master now," he says. "You will wear the collar any time you aren't at the company or performing—all of your private time at home. You will shower in it. You will run errands in it. When your street clothes go on, your collar goes on. You will sleep in it. Do you understand?"

"Yes, Master." It's a whisper, and this time he doesn't ask for more. My fingertips stroke over the thin metal collar. He's slowly seduced me deeper and deeper into this... thing between us. I don't know what this means to him, but whatever it is feels more and more permanent with each passing day.

"Were there really other people here, or was it just us?" I ask.

He doesn't answer. Instead he says, "It's time for your shower."

His footsteps recede. I wait an appropriate length of time and then take the blindfold off. As the water of the shower heats, I stand in front of the mirror, staring at the shiny platinum collar around my throat. The initials *S. T.* are engraved in the front. I simply stare at those letters and ponder this new clue.

11

W eeks go by. Performances and rehearsals. Night after night of masturbating according to his demands, screaming out my pleasure to satisfy his distant lust. The collar around my throat as I sleep. The meetings with him each Wednesday, this erotic fever dream pitching higher and higher. He continues to train my ass, the toys slowly escalating in girth, yet still he doesn't fuck me. Does he not want to fuck me? I can't believe I ask myself this question, that I'm somehow broken by the fact that my black-mailer has refused to breach this final barrier between us.

But it feels like rejection, and I can't help that I'm hurt by it.

I go through my free time out in the world wondering if anyone understands what this piece of jewelry around my throat means.

I've avoided invitations to hang out with Henry and Melinda, begging off with the best excuses I can come up with so I don't hurt their feelings. I don't want them to think I'm snubbing them because I'm a principal now and they're still in the corps. It's not that. It's that I can't bring myself to let them see this metal around my throat—I can't answer the questions I know would come. And I equally can't bring myself to disobey him by not wearing it at the specified times he's demanded.

It's Monday morning, and today we're starting on Firebird. I'm nervous and excited and worried I won't live up to the choreographer's demands as I enter Studio B.

"Ah, Cassia," Mr. V. says, motioning me over to where he stands with a tall broad man wearing a black T-shirt, black pants, and ballet shoes. "I'd like you to meet the guest choreographer. Morgan Elliott."

"Hello," I say.

He stares at me for several seconds, assessing me openly. He has brilliant green eyes and dark hair. Instead of returning my greeting, he simply nods. I break the stare first, looking down.

"Warm up, and we'll get started on the first *pas de deux,*" Mr. V. says. "Morgan wants to see how you and Frederick dance together."

I nod and move to the barre beside Frederick, who is already stretching. He gives me a wink, and I smile back. I'm glad we're dancing together. Frederick has such an easy way that I know I'll feel safe dancing with him.

I chance a glance back to Mr. V. and the choreographer, my heart in my throat. The way he looked at me. His build. His hair color. So much like the man in Mr. V.'s office. And he just nodded. He didn't speak.

Is it *him*? I feel so ridiculous about all the people I've guessed could be the man whose initials are S.T. The choreographer's name doesn't start with these initials, but does that matter? He'll have to speak eventually. It would be too strange if he didn't. And then I'll know for sure. My stomach flutters with a thousand butterflies as I go through my warm-up routine, unsure if I want this man to be him or not.

"Frederick, Cassia," Mr. V. says, calling our attention. "We're ready for you."

Frederick takes my hand and squeezes it briefly. "You'll do great. You're an amazing dancer," he says, misunderstanding the reason for my obvious nerves.

But I'm grateful I can hide behind this misunderstanding. The choreographer continues to watch me as Frederick and I move to the center of the sprung floor, ready to take instruction.

The choreographer picks up a red piece of fabric and comes to stand beside me. Without a word, he ties the scrap of red silk around my eyes. My breathing goes shallow.

"In this ballet, you'll be dancing with a blindfold for part of it. Can you see through the fabric?" the choreographer asks.

I let out a long, slow breath, trying to will my heartbeat to calm back to normal. It's not the same voice. It's not him.

"Y-yes, Sir," I say. I'm not sure if I'm supposed to call him by his name. Guest choreographers don't necessarily follow all the same protocols of the company. But he doesn't comment on my formality.

"Good. The audience will be wowed, but it's more illusion than anything. It won't be as easy as dancing without it, but with practice, you should be able to orient yourself on the stage."

I almost laugh out loud at this. He doesn't know I've been dancing on a stage with a blindfold that isn't just an illusion. This is nothing by comparison.

"Frederick, step back and give her some room," he says.

Morgan turns his attention back to me. "Okay, I want you to try a few *pirouettes*. Use your outline in the mirror to spot."

I do as he asks, doing three sharp, quick turns in succession.

"Wonderful. So you can see well enough, then. You can take the blindfold off for now." I untie the fabric and turn my attention back to the choreographer, trying desperately not to think of the stranger in the theater and all the associations that have attached themselves to blindfolds in the past couple of months.

The choreographer goes on to explain his vision for this Firebird. The blindfold is used as a tool of ensnaring her to Prince Ivan. She doesn't know who has her or what he wants at first. I listen carefully to the new story that has been concocted, and it sounds so much like the story of my own capture.

Just as in the original Firebird, Prince Ivan will only let her go if she promises to return to him when he asks. The choreography is challenging but a pleasure to dance. It's all so fluid, like a dream. I do feel like an actual bird as Frederick and I dance together.

I turn to find a few of the company dancers standing out in the hallway watching through the large picture windows.

When we break for lunch, the choreographer pulls me aside.

"I'm not sure of the company's rules," Morgan says, "But I was wondering if you'd like to have lunch with me."

I gape at him for a moment. In all the initial panic that he might be *him*, it hadn't occurred to me that the way he was looking at me was garden-variety interest. It's been so long since I've had innocent interest aimed at me that it's hard for a moment to think what to do with it.

Morgan is very attractive. And he seems nice. I'm not sure what *S. T.* would say about this, but I'm fairly confident that although he only officially owns me for three hours a week, that dating is not a luxury I'm allowed.

"She's married," Frederick says, saving me from having to navigate the situation. Oh, yeah. I'm married. They don't know about Conall.

"You're awfully young to be so caged," the choreographer remarks.

I blush at this and allow Frederick to pull me away from the awkward situation. My partner has taken a protective interest in me. If only he knew there are far bigger wolves in my life than Morgan Elliott.

I join Frederick and the other principals for lunch at a nice restaurant downtown that has a light lunch menu. We sit outside in the unseasonably warm day next to a burbling fountain eating as birds play and drink the flowing water.

"What do you think of the choreography?" Frederick asks between bites of pasta.

"I like it. I think it's going to be an amazing show."

"It looked fantastic," Natalie says.

"Do you think you'll be comfortable dancing with the blindfold on stage?" Frederick asks.

"Didn't I look comfortable?" Once we were taught the choreography, and I had all the steps down, I started doing the solo with the blindfold, leading into the *pas de deux* with Frederick.

He laughs. "Eerily so."

Yes. Eerie. What a strange coincidence. Not only does the story of the firebird mimic my conditions of captivity, but the blindfold does as well.

12

W hen I arrive at the opera house on Wednesday, I'm wearing one of the charcoal-colored leotards, my hair in a neat bun. I feel the weight of the collar around my throat—the only jewelry he allows me now on this stage. The metal cage that ensnares his firebird.

I warm up at the barre in silence, the bright spotlight shining on me.

"Hello?" I call out when I finish, my voice echoing off the walls. He usually greets me when I arrive. "Master?"

I will never get used to this title he's demanded of me. It thrills and upsets me in equal measure. It elates and shames me all at the same time.

"Take off your clothes. Go to the table. Put on the blindfold, then bend over and rest your hands on the table and wait for me."

I let out a slow breath. I do as my Master commands. Moments after I'm nude with my hands flat on the table, I feel his approach. He strokes my throat, my breast, the flank of my hip.

A moment later, I whimper as cold lubed metal slides into my ass. It's tapered at the top and then flares out at the base so that it fits snugly inside my body. The plug isn't too large. He's penetrated my ass with larger toys before; still, it's so unexpected this early in the night that it takes my body a moment to adjust. He strokes my ass for a few moments.

"Comfortable?" he asks.

"Yes, Master." I'm not sure I would call it that, but I know it pleases him to hear me say these words, so I say them. My arousal is already climbing. Why won't he fuck me?

"Stay," he says. I feel his retreat. Several minutes pass before I hear his voice again over the sound system.

"You can take off the blindfold. Put on the costume and the shoes."

I remove the blindfold to find a gorgeous flaming red costume with layers and layers of wispy material, lying across the table along with a pair of red *pointe* shoes resting on top of the pile of fabric.

I'm about to protest that I need more time because you can't just put on a new pair of *pointe* shoes straight out of the box. As a dancer, he must know that. But as I pick up the shoes from the pile of red material, I see he's already done the requisite ripping of the satin at the toes, the scraping, the beating of the boxes.

I'm sure he's had these made for me in my exact specifications. All this information is on file with the company after all. With every other string he's pulled, getting that information would be nothing.

"You can test them to see if they're how you like them," he says.

The ribbons and elastics aren't sewn in yet. Dancers always

sew these in ourselves. We are very particular about exactly where to put them for our particular feet and comfort.

I slip into the costume even more aware of the plug in my ass, blushing at the thought of dancing this way. The fairy-like costume fits me like a glove. I twirl in it. "It's beautiful. Is this for the show?"

"No, cupcake. It's simply a gift. I'm not in charge of costuming. I don't have *that* much power."

I actually laugh at this.

I try the shoes and test them, surprised that I'm happy with how he's broken them in. I try to imagine him sitting on the stage before I got here, beating the toe boxes against the floor. The image in my mind is comical.

I sit on the stage and sew the elastics and ribbons in. Then I put the shoes on and do a few experimental *tendus*, jumps, and *pirouettes*. Everything is as it should be.

"Good girl. Now go to the barre and put the blindfold on."

I obey his orders, trying to calm the excitement rising within me.

A few minutes later, he's beside me again, his hand kneading the back of my neck. I lean into him, a soft moan leaving my mouth.

"We're going to do the *pas de deux* you learned this week for Firebird," he says.

"Do you know it?" I ask, shocked that he would.

He laughs. "Know it? Of course I know it. I choreographed it."

I stiffen even though I know the choreographer's voice was different. It wasn't him. I know it wasn't him.

"He doesn't have the same voice as you." I can't help voicing my small doubt.

"No, I'm not the man you met Monday. I taught the chore-ography to someone who is now teaching it to you."

"Are you ever going to let me see you?" There is a kind of comfort behind the blindfold. But still, I want to see him. "I-I won't tell anyone."

He has to know we are well beyond the possibility that the revelation of his identity to me could pose any threat to him. But he doesn't respond to my question.

We dance. Almost every movement creates greater aware-ness of the toy he pushed inside my ass.

I try to imagine what I must look like on this stage in this swirling fire costume and red shoes, and the black blindfold. When the music stops, we're breathing hard. I want to reach out and touch him so badly, but I know he'll never let me see his face even with only my hands.

I try not to let it bother me, this fuzzy layer between us, the guard he always keeps up. I want him to trust me. I need him to let me in. His mouth is on mine suddenly in a feverish demanding kiss that takes my breath from me. I gasp into his mouth. He rips the costume off me, and I can't stop the tears.

"I... I loved that..."

"I'll buy you a new one," he snarls, impatiently shoving my tights down past my hips. He picks me up and carries me a distance away. I shriek when he drops me, but the soft mattress catches my fall, and I didn't fall far anyway.

And then he is on me, his teeth biting and scraping at the sensitive flesh of my throat just above my collar. He grips the platinum band and pulls me closer to him, his mouth again finding mine, then he shoves me away, and I fall on my back on the mattress.

He curses as he struggles to untie the knots of the ribbons helping to bind the red shoes to my feet. "Goddammit," he says again. I think he'll destroy my shoes too, but he finally gets one off, then the other. I hear them crash against the stage far away where he tosses them.

He violently rips the tights off me. His own clothes follow in a flurry of zipper and pulling of fabric and tossing of clothing away. A blissful sigh leaves my mouth as he sheathes himself inside me.

I knew he was big, but the feel of him this way is the most exquisite burn of pleasure and fullness. As he moves inside me, the toy in my ass shifts as well.

"Who do you belong to?" he growls as he fucks me. His arms are wrapped around me, completely enveloping me. I feel like his firebird, trapped, helpless and hopeless with no choice but to dance to his tune.

"You, Master."

I wonder if he knows about the choreographer asking me out and what happened after. I wonder if he put him up to it to test me and see what I would do—just another spy. Just another camera lens watching me and reporting back to my master.

Will he become like Conall? Possessive and trapping? I struggle in his arms, feeling smothered, afraid that he is my new Conall. Will I have to kill him, too? How could I ever? He plans everything so carefully, his guard is never down. And I need him. I want him. The things he makes me feel... I could never...

His mouth kisses and sucks against my throat, and I come undone in his arms, my pleasure flowing out of me in a long wave. He thrusts one final time inside me, the movement so harsh, it's like a brand on my flesh, like he's trying to permanently mark me with his cock.

He takes the toy out of my ass then falls on top of me, holding me, and I start to cry.

He rolls off of me but doesn't leave. He strokes my hair. "What's wrong, cupcake?"

"Are you going to get jealous and possessive if another man looks at me? Are you going to make threats and... like Conall... please... I can't do it again. Please..."

"Shhh," his fingertips trail over my cheek, wiping my tears, then he moves down, fingering my collar, then stroking small circles over my breasts.

"I'm not threatened," he says. "I know you'll always fly back to your cage to me. You're such a very good girl."

"The choreographer asked me out for lunch," I say.

He doesn't stop his gentle caresses. His fingers don't pause or stutter over my skin. "Did you go?" he asks.

"N-no. Frederick told him I was married."

He chuckles. "Frederick makes a good guard dog. Would you have gone?"

I shake my head. He doesn't comment on this. He doesn't call me a liar or make threats or shout about how he'll fucking kill the choreographer. He just stands and pulls me up with him. Then he carries me back in the direction from which we came.

He sits me down on the chair at the table.

"Stay. Leave the blindfold on," he orders.

He returns a few moments later, and I hear a large cap unscrew, and then a liquid being poured. A spoon prods at my lips.

"Open, cupcake. You sounded like you were getting sick yesterday. I need you healthy for rehearsals. I can't let you come down with anything."

It's warm, soothing chicken soup. It tastes homemade, like the other things he's fed me.

"Did you make this?" I ask.

"I make everything," he says. And there are so many layers of meaning in this simple statement.

As he's feeding me, I wonder how he knows I sounded like I was getting sick yesterday. Is the choreographer reporting back to him? Does he have recording devices? Another spy? I don't know, and it takes too much energy to care.

So I just let him take care of me.

13

W eeks more have passed, and I've given up the hope that he'll ever truly let me into his world.

The Firebird opens on a Sunday night. I'm so nervous. I can't fucking stand this. I need the curtain to open. I need to start. Once I get out there, I know I'll be fine. I've never been this nervous in my entire life. I've been on this stage performing four nights a week during the season for years now.

But being in the corps, you can pretend no one pays attention to you. If you mess up, chances are most people didn't notice. Their eyes were on another dancer—usually one of the principals. But tonight, it's all about me. It's all on me.

A weight of responsibility settles on my shoulders, and I suddenly understand why there's such a strict hierarchy in the ballet world. I understand now why Natalie and Frederick command the respect they do from the entire company. It's because the weight of all of our jobs to some degree rests on them. All the principals carry this weight.

The strength of the company rests on their talent, and not

just their innate talent but what they actually bring to the stage when the pressure is on. Suddenly, I feel unready for this. I've dreamed and dreamed and wished on every candle and star in my path for ages, and yet now... what if I fuck this up? What if I'm not ready?

It doesn't matter if I'm the best dancer in the corps. What were they thinking putting me in this role? We aren't supposed to, but I peek through the edge of the curtains to the box where I'm back to being convinced that my mysterious lover, benefactor, and tormentor sits at every performance. But he's not out there. He's not here.

Maybe he's running late. Or maybe he's never here until right before the curtain rises. I don't know; I've never stolen a peek before the show like this before.

Panic surges through me. I need him here. He doesn't make me nervous or distract me. He makes me feel grounded, anchored to this plane of reality. And he's not here. The theater is packed. Whispers of the new and exciting Firebird choreography and the new principal dancer have swept through the city, and probably the larger ballet world as well.

I'm going to die. I cannot do this. Then a hand is in mine. Frederick spins me around to face him. "Hey. You've got this. You'll do great. And I'll be out there with you. Old pro here, remember?" He winks at me, charming as ever.

I nod, managing a weak smile. The orchestra starts warming up. Oh god, I'm going to die.

"Breathe," Frederick says. "Do you want to run the first part again?"

I shake my head. "It's too late. We don't have time."

"You know this. It's all in your muscles. Don't think. Just let it happen. You do this every week."

I do not do *this* every week. This is very much a different thing from what I've been doing every week. It's a special sort of tragedy that I'm only realizing this now, moments before going onstage.

A few minutes later, the music starts, and I go on. Once I'm out there, the nerves do diminish. I feel the energy of the audience feeding me, supporting each leap and each turn. I relax into the role. I'm no longer Cassia. I am the firebird, and somehow I know everyone in the audience and in the company knows it. If there was a single doubt about me, it's erased in my opening solo. As I move, I feel a heat rise off me as if I'm made of actual flame. It's a living energy, and I'm sure right now that the audience can see this, too.

At the end of my solo, I glance up at the box, and my heart sinks to find it empty. He's not coming, I realize. I fight back the tears that he isn't here to see this. Did I do something wrong? Did something happen? Is he hurt somewhere?

I can't stop the endless chattering in my mind, even as Frederick's promise that my muscles will remember proves true. They don't let me down. Frederick has an introductory solo, and then there's a piece from the corps.

Then I'm on stage again in my favorite scene in this re-imagined Firebird, the capture. The audience gasps at my blindfold. It wouldn't occur to them that of course I can see through this material. Not well, but I can see enough.

I move easily through my part. I'm nervous again about the leaps. I remember being pushed in the old opera house through *grand jetés* across the floor, and I'm worried it won't be spectacular enough. It won't be dramatic enough. I won't do this choreography justice. But he isn't in the audience anyway. This performance doesn't have to please him. He won't punish me for any missteps. And I've already won the hearts and minds of everyone who is watching.

But I'm still so hurt. He isn't here to watch me perform his choreography. Why wouldn't he be here?

The music changes, and I feel Frederick behind me. Then his hands are on my waist and the *pas de deux* begins.

But it isn't Frederick. It's *him*. I would know his hands on me anywhere. This is not how Frederick dances. The difference in dance partners is absolute and distinct. He guides me through the dance, the blindfold still in place.

The orchestra reaches a crescendo, and he rips the blindfold off and turns me to face him. It's all in the choreography, but it's also so much more. I see him, and I flinch. I know him. I know who this man is. His dark intense gaze ensnares mine.

I have to fight the gasp, though I don't know why I should. The audience will eat this up, thinking this is some amazing acting ability on my part. He pulls me in toward him and says, "Don't disappoint me, Firebird." He propels me away from him, launching me in a series of spins and turns.

Then I run. Not off the stage. In the choreography, I run from him. *Run run run grand jeté across the stage.* But he's there, ready for me. Then the other direction. *Run run run grand jeté across the stage.* But he's there. He captures me, and we dance together. Each lift is precise. Each turn sharp and perfect.

He never wavers in his support, and I do everything in my power not to think about who he is because I'm on a stage, and there's no room for being anything other than the firebird in this moment.

The *pas de deux* ends, and with it, the scene. I'm locked in his embrace. We're staring at each other, breathing hard. It isn't customary for an audience to give a standing ovation during the middle of a performance. But the people who have become spellbound by me and my partner do not care. They've lost all sense of propriety and etiquette. They've been swept away by this primal act played out before their greedy eyes in the glare of the spotlight.

Everything they know about the appropriate time to clap, the appropriate time to stand... It all fades away. The orchestra has to actually stop, and there's silence except for this thundering applause. It goes on forever.

No one seems to care that my dance partner was just switched out mid-performance. No one has missed a single stride. Not me, not my new partner, and not the audience.

He leads me off the stage, and before I can question him or say anything, I'm engulfed by the other dancers in the wings as he slips away. Congratulations and excited exclamations about how magical that was pour over me in a wave. They gush about how they've never seen anything like it.

I look around, but I can't find him now. He's disappeared somewhere into the shadows like the phantom of the fucking opera. What about our next scene? Will it be Frederick back on stage again? How will the audience react to that?

"Oh. My. God!" Henry says. He's not in this next scene, so he pulls me back away from the wings out of the way of another string of dancers who are about to go on. "Oh my God," he says again. "Do you know who that was? Do you know who you just danced with? Oh my God."

I nod, my body shaking from all the adrenaline. Yes. I know who I just danced with. Sebastian Trent. He was possibly the top male dancer in the entire ballet world—and I mean internationally—until a motorcycle accident ended his career a couple of years ago. No one saw him after that. He just disappeared.

And I understand why. While he dances as beautifully as he ever did, he has a severe scar on his face that makes him look intense and frightening. I couldn't help the flinch.

"Are you sleeping with him?" Henry asks.

"W-what?" I have to fight not to shriek that. There *is* a live performance going on just yards away after all. And I have to go back on soon. Someone hands me my next costume, and I start stripping down while Henry helps me change and continues to talk.

"I mean... I'm sorry, but that looked like fucking on stage. It was seriously intense. That kind of chemistry doesn't just happen. Are you seeing him? Have you danced with him before?"

"I..." I don't even know what to say to this. So I don't say anything. I don't have time anyway. Instead, I ask, "Where's Frederick? We have to go back on in two minutes."

"He fell and hurt his ankle. He's on the way to the hospital."

"What about the understudy? Who the fuck am I dancing with?" I hiss.

I haven't practiced this recently with the understudy. I don't know how to do the rest of this performance with the understudy. I move to the wings, and nobody has miraculously appeared. Moments before we're supposed to go back on, someone is behind me, his hand in mine.

It's Sebastian. I let out a sigh.

He doesn't say anything to me; he just leads me out on stage, and we dance. We dance the rest of the ballet together. Maybe the director and choreographer thought it would be a bad idea to have three different Prince Ivans for one opening performance. Besides, the audience might have launched a full-scale mutiny if Sebastian didn't return to them. So deep is their love for him... and the thrill of his unexpected return to the stage.

If they noticed the scar, they don't care about it. If I

thought the standing ovation after our initial scene together went on forever, the one at the end of the ballet goes on so long I actually want them to stop because I'm getting hungry. I need to eat. I need to rest. I need to be off this stage. And I need to talk to Sebastian. Maybe not in that order.

Actual roses are thrown on the stage. I've seen this happen a few times before, but it's usually at really high profile performances. Though I guess we just became high profile. New Firebird and Sebastian Trent all in one night. There's a sense of breathlessness in the air about all this.

As we take our final bows, Sebastian's gaze locks with mine. His intense expression is inscrutable. I wish I knew what he was thinking right now. He grips my hand so tightly, and for a moment, I'm not sure whether he'll take me away and lock me in a tower, or if he'll slip out of my grasp forever.

When we get off stage, Sebastian runs. Like *runs*. He moves so fucking fast I could never hope to catch him. In this moment, I'm so afraid I'll never see him again, but I'm swept up again in a chorus of cheers and congratulations. Henry drags me to the opening night after party. And of course, Sebastian isn't there. He is a ghost.

14

It's Wednesday night. I've barely eaten anything the past two days. The company hasn't settled down from the buzz of excitement over Sebastian's mysterious appearance at the show followed by his subsequent disappearance and what it might mean and if he'll be joining the company, and what in the fuck is actually going on?

Literally everyone has asked if I'm sleeping with him. This question has made me blush more times than I can count because clearly that entire audience had some sort of voyeuristic experience with Sebastian and me. If everyone in the company thinks we're sleeping together, then the audience definitely did. It feels as though they've intruded on our privacy, our intimate moments on our private stage.

I've spent the past two days rehearsing with Shane, the understudy for Prince Ivan. Shane is nice enough, and he's a good dancer, but he isn't Frederick. And he's definitely not Sebastian. But I'm polite and professional, and when he nearly dropped me on a lift yesterday, I bit back the urge to scream at him—to ask if he wanted me in the hospital, too! Difficult prima donna is not a good look, and I don't want to become a ballet monster before Natalie's spot at the barre is even cold.

I've asked Mr. V. and Morgan about Frederick. When he's coming back. How long he has to be off the foot. When he can dance again... but they've been tight-lipped. No one is talking about it.

I reach the old Opera house a few minutes before nine. The spotlight lights up the stage and the barre as usual. But there's silence. It's a silence so loud and oppressive I find myself looking over my shoulder, wondering whether I'm alone, wondering if someone else or something else might lurk in the shadows watching me instead of the man I'm hoping to find.

"Sebastian!" I call out. It's the first time I've spoken his name out loud. No answer. He's not here. I feel a tear sliding down my cheek at the thought that he would abandon me after everything. Why? Because I saw his face? What difference can that possibly make now?

"Sebastian, are you here? Please, answer me."

I walk down the darkened aisle and climb the steps of the stage. I'm about to get ready for our weekly ritual, but I don't know which shoes to wear. I don't know which he wants. I don't even know if I'm alone right now. A choked sob escapes my throat, and I crumple to the ground and start to cry.

His voice booms over the speaker. "I'm surprised you're here."

I look up and around, as I always do, never quite sure where he actually is. I feel relief. "Of course I'm here," I say. "I have to come here or you'll ruin my life."

He chuckles at that. "Oh, Ms. Lane. That's not why you

come here. You knew after the first few weeks I wouldn't report you."

"I did not!" Did I know that? I'd stopped thinking about it or caring about it because I started to crave this... thing between us. This secret.

"You kept coming here because you need this. You need the pain. You need the judgment. You need my eyes on you, demanding your obedience. You dance to obey. You stand at that barre every day obeying the commands of the ballet master because you need that thrill you get when you please him."

"It's not sexual." But I don't deny the rest of it. There's no point. That's why I dance. I need the control. I need someone else besides me to be in control and tell me what to do. I need to just worry about executing the steps perfectly and nothing more. I need the peaceful space it creates inside my brain.

Another chuckle. "Isn't it? Isn't it just another kink, cupcake? I took your dark little needs out of the shadows and made them explicit. I made you exist for me on my stage. And you kept coming back for more because I saw you. I saw what you needed, and I gave it to you. But if I'd met you in any normal way, you would never have done it. You needed permission. You needed just a little threat to push you over the edge into my arms."

I don't have an answer to any of this. I know he's right. And if he could read me so easily, could others? I'm blushing furiously now.

"There's nothing to be ashamed of. Most dancers are masochists. Did you know ballerinas have a pain threshold three times higher than the general population? I wonder if that's training or if it's self-selecting. Maybe only the strong survive. That's why you were drawn to Conall."

"No! I never wanted him to hurt me." I don't care who Sebastian is or how much power he has to destroy me, he will *not* imply that I somehow asked for the things Conall did to me. The way he hurt me, abused my trust, made me live in so much panic that the only safety for me was the sanctuary of the studio or the stage—where everything was controlled and nothing was unpredictable.

"Shhhh. I know. You thought you saw a kind of dominance that you needed. It's so easy for the young and uninitiated to think they see dominance when it's really just abuse. I know what you need. But if I had come to you, you would have run from me. You would have taken one look at my scarred face and..."

"It doesn't make you ugly," I say. And it doesn't. His photograph used to be splashed across every dance magazine in the world. So I know what Sebastian Trent looked like before the accident that ended his career, but the scars don't lessen his beauty. I guess there's a level of attractive nothing can touch.

"But they make me look dangerous. And after Conall, you never would have come to me on your own."

I sigh. I can't deny it. That's probably true. And he does look dangerous. He looks lethal. Not that I can see him right now. He's hidden in whatever shadowy nook he lurks in.

But though he may look dangerous, his hands on me feel like home. Is that why he thought I wouldn't show up tonight? That look on my face on stage? That flinch?

Did he think it was revulsion? That all my little fantasies were shattered in a moment at the reality of the scars marring his perfection? Did he think the world he'd created for us on this secret stage was shattered now as clean beautiful lines were replaced by sharp broken ones?

"What happened Sunday? How did you end up on stage

with me?" I ask because I have to know. No one knew much the night of the performance, and the decision makers at the company who do know seem to have taken a vow of silence on the issue.

Even though Sebastian is a disembodied voice, even though he's still hiding from me, our typical formality is broken in the wake of this revelation which I haven't been able to stop thinking about for three days.

"I was backstage, careful not to draw attention to myself. I stayed in the shadows and out of your path. I wanted to watch your first principal performance from the wings. There are so many unique things to see from that vantage point: your quick costume changes, you working through your nerves before going onstage, your elation coming off stage, words of congratulations and great job from the other dancers waiting in the wings to go on. It's something I can't get from a box seat."

I warm up at the barre in my soft canvas ballet shoes as he speaks.

"Frederick was showing off in the wings five fucking minutes before he was supposed to join you on stage. He fell and broke his ankle, though we didn't know it was broken at the time. He's out for the season. The understudy couldn't be found with only minutes to go on stage. I was there. I knew the part. I wasn't going to just leave you out there without a partner. I made Frederick strip and took the costume. Apparently while we were dancing, the paramedics took him out of there naked. I was fucking furious, so I hardly cared. And you know the rest. We danced."

What we did was so much more than dance. My breath catches in my throat at the memory of the moment when his hands spanned my waist with such certainty I knew exactly who had me.

"I-I didn't know you could still dance," I say.

"Of course you did. You've been dancing with me for months."

"But I didn't know it was you. I thought you retired because you were too injured."

Sebastian sighs. "There was a lot of rehabilitation, and I'm not sure I'm quite back where I was technique-wise. But it was mostly the scars on my face. It's not exactly a ballet aesthetic. You know? And I didn't want pity or people to come see me out of some morbid fascination like some sideshow freak."

I understand this. The world of ballet is all about beauty and the illusion of perfection. A beautiful top male principal dancer, lusted after by nearly everyone who watches him, suffers a disfiguring accident... There's pity and shock. And he's going back on stage? Not in this lifetime. I get it.

"Who will I be dancing with for the rest of the season?" I ask. I don't hate the understudy, but I'm not nearly as comfortable with Shane as I am with Frederick on stage.

"Me," he says. "Apparently, after Sunday night, you and I are the talk of the dance world. So, I guess I'm back."

"The company hired you?"

He laughs. "I own controlling interest in the company. Trent is a name I invented to perform under and hide my family money. My real name is Sebastian Grant of Grant Enterprises. After I retired, I found this company struggling and offered to help. I wasn't planning on performing again, even though I was asked to. Now, after Sunday night, people are a lot more insistent."

A giddy thrill runs through me at the prospect of being partnered on stage with THE Sebastian Trent for the rest of the season.

"But if you're dancing with me, why have I been rehearsing with the understudy the past two days?"

I can almost hear the shrug in his voice. "Because it took the company that long to convince me to come out of retirement. I'll be dancing with you tomorrow night."

Sebastian Trent and me, up on the big marquee in front of the theater for the entire run of the Firebird.

"Put the blindfold on," he says.

"But, I've seen you."

"This isn't a negotiation, Ms. Lane; put it on."

"Yes, Master," slips past my lips as I reach for the scrap of black fabric hanging over the barre. I can almost feel his smile from wherever he is. It permeates the air like a hot breath during a slow fuck.

A few minutes later, he's beside me. He takes my hand and slings my dance bag over my shoulder.

"Step down," he says when we reach the stairs at the side of the stage. I tentatively feel my way down each step. "Where are we going?"

But he says nothing. He just leads me up the aisle and out through the concession area. I only know because of the way the sound of his shoes change when we go from carpet to hard floor. Then outside into the cold night.

My breathing is coming harder as unease winds its way through me. I hear a double beep on a car, and a door opens.

"Get in," he says. He helps me into the car, then shuts and locks me inside. My hand reaches out instinctively for the door, but the child locks are on.

A moment later, the other door opens, the locks snap down again, and the car starts up. I reach to remove the blindfold, becoming increasingly panicked by this change in our pattern.

He grips my wrist, hard. "No."

A moment later, a rope is being tied around my wrists and then looped and tied around my hands so I can't remove the blindfold. I'm crying now. I can't help it. I'm scared. I haven't been this scared of him in a long time.

Sebastian's identity is no longer a mystery, but somehow he seems wilder now. Because I've seen his face. What if he's decided I'm a threat? But if that were true, he would never have let me out of his sight. He wouldn't be talking like we're going to dance together.

I know I'm being crazy, but being bound and blindfolded in his car while he drives us to god knows where makes it hard to think rationally. What if he just takes me out into the woods somewhere, kills me, and dumps my body? It's not as though I'm the only person he can dance with in his big ballet come-back. Even though I thought it was special between us, maybe he doesn't feel the same.

Maybe he's crazy. He's obviously crazy. He blackmailed me. He's made me do all these things... for weeks... blindfolded... How could I have allowed myself to trust this man even for a moment? How could I have allowed myself to forget the way this all started? This is not a man playing by the rules of society, so why do I think he wouldn't hurt me? Conall hurt me! I lived with that and danced with that for three years. So maybe he won't kill me... but that doesn't mean he won't hurt me.

"Please, tell me where you're taking me. I-I'm not going to say anything. I swear. Please, Master, I swear. I won't tell anyone about anything..." I trail off because I'm becoming increasingly afraid that the more I talk the more he may begin to see me as a bigger threat.

We drive for what seems like forever. He is silent. He

doesn't try to calm me. He doesn't reassure me that I'm safe. Why won't he reassure me that I'm safe? Because I'm not!

They say don't let an attacker take you to a second location. Is he an attacker? Is that what he is to me? My body hasn't seemed to think so. In fact, until this exact moment, my body has treated him like a welcome lover, not a potential true threat.

And wasn't the opera house technically the *second location*? So are we going to the third location now? Is that worse? Where the fuck is he taking me?

"Master? H-how did you know about what I did to Conall?"

I can't believe I've never asked this question. I've been so consumed with keeping my secret that I haven't pushed him for answers. But now things feel so precarious. It feels like I'm about to die. And if that's true, I need to know these things. I wait in the dark silence of the car, thinking he won't answer, but finally he speaks.

"I saw him getting aggressive with you earlier that day outside the company. I pulled your file from the computer and went to your house that evening. I was about to ring the doorbell when I saw him stumbling to the bathroom through one of the front windows. I watched the rest and followed you from there."

"W-what were you going to do when you came over?" I need him to keep talking.

But he doesn't answer me. Silence descends, and I start crying again. Why won't he talk to me? Why is he taking me off site?

I keep telling myself over and over that he's not going to take me somewhere and kill me. Why would he? He knows I won't report him. And wouldn't it look suspicious if I just disappeared?

"A-are you done with me?" I ask. "Please... you said if I did what you said... u-until you were done that you would let me go. You said you wouldn't report me and..." I'm rambling now. I'm so fucking terrified. I can't seem to rationalize my way out of this fear.

"No, cupcake. I'm far from done with you," he says.

I hold onto this endearment even though I'm unsure if him not being done with me is a good thing or not.

Finally the car stops. I flinch when his car door slams. It has a sort of echo-y quality—like we're in a parking garage. This causes me to tense. Why would he bring me to an abandoned parking garage? Is it abandoned?

He opens my door, and before I can protest, he's scooped me up in his arms and is carrying me. I hear a ding and a metal door slide open.

"Service elevator," he says.

Service elevator to what?? Are we at his house? What is going on?

"You're scaring me," I whisper when the doors close, and the elevator begins its steady lurch upward.

He grips me tighter in his arms. "I know."

All I can think is that he likes keeping me on edge. He likes my fear. He likes forcing me into situations where I have no choice but to trust and rely on him. And now that I've seen his face, he's finding new ways to raise the stakes. Why? How far will he raise them, and will I come out of this alive?

My crying is louder, and I swear he doesn't seem to care. What happened to the man I was starting to trust even though I couldn't see him? The way he held me on stage, his *shhh you're safe.*

I realize suddenly that for the first time since we started this, tonight when he told me to put the blindfold on, I didn't have the normal excited reaction. Too much hung in the air. I had too many questions.

And now both my body and mind are finally in accord. They both see this man as a threat. Does he now see me the same way?

"Are you angry with me? Did I do something wrong? Master, please..."

He presses a finger to my lips. "Shhh."

But that's all he says. Why is he doing this?

The elevator stops. The doors open. He carries me down a hallway, unlocks a door, and then takes me inside... wherever we are.

He sits me down in a hard chair and begins untying the ropes around my wrists and hands, still silent.

Finally, I can't help it. I have to know. "Are you going to kill me?"

He actually laughs at this. "Of course not. Why would I kill you?"

"You're being weird. I know who you are. You're scaring me. I don't understand..."

He presses a finger to my lips. "Do not speak. I still own you. You have lost all but the barest hint of etiquette between us. I want you back the way you were. I want you perfectly obedient. Just the way I like."

This makes some small measure of sense, that he's trying to get us back to this state we were in before I saw his face.

He wipes tears off my cheeks, and my breathing starts to return to normal. I want to know where we are, why he took me somewhere else. Is this his place? But I'm afraid if I ask these questions, he'll be disappointed. I want to earn his *shhh, you're safe*. I need it.

He takes my hands in his, helps me to stand, and guides me through the room. I suddenly have that eerie feeling again, like I'm being watched. That feeling I got that day in the theater when he made me believe for the smallest moment that someone else was there with us, watching the things he did to me on that stage.

Music starts from a sound system across the room. A piano concerto. Sebastian stands behind me, his voice a low growl in my ear. "Take your clothes off for our guest."

"Bastian, for fuck's sake. She's terrified."

I freeze. I know that voice. It's Morgan.

"You said you wanted to see her cry, that you like her when she's a little afraid," Sebastian says. "I aim to please." He removes my blindfold, and Morgan is giving me that assessing stare, the same one from the day we met, the same one I've caught him giving me in rehearsals.

And now I know Sebastian wasn't just fucking with me that day when he said I had an audience. Morgan has been watching from the darkness of the theater. He's been watching everything. My brain is still struggling to catch up with this new revelation.

That look... it wasn't assessing. It was *knowing.* All this time I've thought Sebastian and I shared a secret, but there was a larger secret I wasn't in on.

"You wanted to go with him when he asked you out for lunch, didn't you?" Sebastian asks.

"N-no," I protest, even though it might be a lie. I'm not sure. I was caught off guard. Morgan is quite good-looking. But Conall's jealousy is a hard thing to forget, and it feels too risky to give Sebastian honesty right now. I'm still so afraid he'll hurt me. I'm afraid he's the same kind of monster I already killed.

"No, what?" Sebastian says, his finger hooking into the platinum band of my collar to remind me that he is not Sebastian to me. He isn't even Sir anymore.

"I..." I look to Morgan as if he can save me.

"Say it," Morgan says, a greedy voyeurism in his eyes. "I want to hear you say it."

I turn back to Sebastian, unable to look at Morgan when I say the word, even though I know he's heard me when I thought Sebastian and I were alone. "No, Master," I whisper.

"I'm never going to be done with you, cupcake. You're moving in. Here, with me and my brother. We're going to share you." His tone is completely nonchalant. As if this is a normal thing to say.

I look back and forth between the two men, for the first time seeing the resemblance in their features. I saw the similarity in their build and hair color the day I met Morgan. It was why I was so sure he was my blackmailer until he spoke.

"You can't be brothers. You don't have the same last name." I must sound like such an idiot, or like a child trying to figure out whodunit in her first Nancy Drew mystery.

"This might shock you, cupcake, but many people use aliases. A lot of people want to hide their family name when there's too much money behind it that might draw unwanted attention."

I finally look around at my surroundings. We're in a huge modern penthouse, with giant floor-to-ceiling windows along one wall. The view is gorgeous, the city lights twinkling in the distance.

Morgan moves closer and presses a kiss against my throat, his hand slipping underneath the gray leotard to stroke my breast. "Be calm, little rabbit. We won't hurt you... much." He pinches my nipple.

The arousal that fled in the face of my fears over what Sebastian might do with me has sparked back to life at this man's touch. I moan. I can't help myself. I don't want to think about what this says about me.

"He's been hogging you for too long," Morgan says.

"Oh, shut up, you got to touch her, too." Sebastian sounds exasperated.

"Not nearly enough," he murmurs as he kisses a trail over my collarbone.

My body goes rigid. Morgan touched me? Does he mean outside of rehearsal? I close my eyes, thinking about all the things that have happened between me and Sebastian in the opera house. All the times he's touched me in different ways. Were some of those times Morgan?

"I fed you the cupcake," he whispers in my ear in answer to my unspoken question. "That was my finger you sucked the frosting off of. But Bastian made it. He's always been better in the kitchen."

I feel so aroused right now but also so betrayed. The tears come again, and I wrench free of Morgan's grasp. I back away from the two of them. I think back to all the things that happened in the theater, trying to reconfigure my memories to account for two men instead of one.

"W-which times was it you?" I ask Morgan. I can't keep my voice from shaking.

I know all the dancing was Sebastian. I know all the orders came from Sebastian's lips.

"I stroked you that first day on the mattress," Morgan says. "Bastian and I took turns getting you off. And I waxed you that day on the stage after your punishment."

"Who fucked me?" I blurt out.

"That was me," Sebastian says. "Morgan hasn't had that pleasure yet."

"Yet?!" I shriek, hysterical. "Fuck yet! You're both insane."

They advance on me, and I back away until I'm pressed against the floor-to-ceiling windows. I look behind me at what would be a precarious drop if we were outside. Still, the height makes me dizzy, and I have to shut my eyes for a moment to steady myself.

"I believe we had an agreement," Sebastian says. "The small matter of the price of my silence."

"OUR silence," Morgan says, happy to insert himself into all my memories after the fact.

I look back and forth between the two of them. "You'd really turn me in? After everything?" I'm crying again. I just can't fucking stop crying. Sebastian just got through telling me tonight that I knew he wasn't going to report me after our first few meetings. Did I? If that's so, why are they making the threat now?

Both men just stare at me, and I have no idea what their stony expressions mean. They won't tell the police. They won't. They get off on this too much. The way they've used me, fucked with me, lied to me. And yet... my body is betraying me.

My body is screaming at my mind, telling it to shut the fuck up and just enjoy this. Because the idea of their hands on me elicits the deepest, most carnal need I've ever felt. I want them to take me together. And I'm so ashamed that I want this.

They're both so beautiful. And masculine. And... frightening. And it isn't Sebastian's scar that makes it so. It's the unapologetic ruthless nature of these two men.

"What else have you done?" I ask Morgan.

"I've kissed you. Some nights I was the one who slid the toy inside your ass."

I whimper at the memories.

Morgan takes this as encouragement and continues, his voice going low and gravelly. "Sometimes when my brother was fucking your mouth, I was the one stroking your cheek, encouraging you."

I don't know what to say to this. I don't know what to feel. So I just stare at him.

"You belong to both of us now," Sebastian says. "Morgan's initials will be added to your collar, and you will call us both Master from now on. You will obey both of us. That's the price of our silence."

"How long?" I ask, an echo of that first night. But I know before he says it. Still... some perverse part of me needs to hear their intention spoken aloud.

"Forever," Sebastian says.

I look to Morgan, whose bright green eyes are so intense I have to look away again. I look back to Sebastian, and then back to Morgan, unsure which man is more dangerous, which is more safe. Who should I appeal to?

"Please..." I don't know why I'm begging. I don't know what I'm begging for, but suddenly I'm one hundred percent sure that it doesn't matter what my body wants right now... I can't do this.

I can't be their slave. They can't take everything from me and expect me to smile pretty and take their cocks like a good girl. I crumple to the ground, my legs no longer willing to support me.

I kneel on the hardwood floor, sobbing. "Please... please please..." I beg. "Please just let me go." Another part of me is screaming *no I want to stay*. But what difference do my conflicting desires make if I don't want them to send me to prison?

Someone is sitting on the ground beside me, pulling me into his arms.

"Shhh, little rabbit," Morgan says. He's petting my hair. "I think we should give her some space to process things. Let her go home... just for a few nights."

I look up, my vision blurred from my tears, to see Sebastian is considering this. They know I'm not going to report them. They have more power. They have the better card to play. The justice system won't absolve me because of their blackmail. Their crimes aren't as high as premeditated murder, and they have enough money and power to buy their freedom from anything anyway.

"Very well," Sebastian finally says, his eyes never leaving mine. "I'll take you home. You can have a few more nights in your own bed. Are you going to be able to dance tomorrow or do we need to use the understudy?"

Oh yeah. I'm dancing with him. How can I dance with him? But I nod my head quickly. "Don't call the understudy. Please, I can dance." I just got this role; I can't lose it now.

"We'll see," Sebastian says, skeptical.

I pull out of Morgan's arms and crawl the few feet over to Sebastian. "Please, Master, I want to dance." He absently strokes my hair.

"Get up, I'll take you home."

I struggle to stand, and Sebastian leads me out of the penthouse, to the service elevator, back to his car. We are silent on the drive. When he pulls up in the circular driveway in front of my house, he finally speaks.

"You belong to us. We won't be moved. Neither of us. So

don't think you can play us against one another. Take this time to make peace with your fate."

I only nod, willing the tears not to start up again. I take my ballet bag and get out of the car without a backward glance.

Once safely locked inside my house, I slide to the floor and sob. By the time I finally drag myself to bed, I'm exhausted, but I can't sleep. I masturbate five times, because it's what I do when I have insomnia.

I try not to think about anything in particular. It's just for comfort. But even I don't believe this lie. Now the fantasies have two men. My body betrays me over and over as I stroke myself to orgasm, my moan filling the darkened room.

15

For four nights, Sebastian and I dance the Firebird. Each night when he rips off the blindfold, revealing himself to me, it feels just as shocking as the first time. Each time, I flinch at his intense expression, that scar. Each time I run from him and leap across the stage. And each time he recaptures me.

The audience is addicted to us. We are a drug to them. Each night, the applause is more thunderous. On Sunday night, when Sebastian ripped the blindfold off, in the quick beat of silence after the orchestral crescendo, I heard an audible gasp in the audience. This is how transfixed they are.

I'm dancing with a man I used to stupidly fantasize about when I first became a professional dancer. Even though he didn't dance at the same company, it didn't stop my stubborn willful wishing mind. I half-believe every candle and wishing star had a second wish enfolded inside the first, that I attached Sebastian to that childish magic, and somehow he appeared. Somehow the magic worked.

Only now I don't know if I can take him. I thought he was larger-than-life before I knew him, but now even that vision seems so small.

He goes out with us after the performances, sitting beside me, holding my hand, confirming that yes, in fact we are seeing each other. The gossip about Conall fleeing the country has finally filtered down through the company.

The other principals say they didn't like him anyway. I'm suddenly ashamed that some part of them knew Conall was hurting me. Can they similarly detect the nature of my relationship with Sebastian?

In my dreams, I'm the firebird. Always trying to fly away, always being captured again by the impossible-to-escape Prince Ivan. In the dream, we are on stage, dancing while Morgan watches. Then we are fucking on the stage while Morgan watches.

I wake from this dream Monday morning, my heart thundering wildly in my chest, an undeniably strong arousal flaring to life between my legs. Even though I've seen Sebastian every night for our show, it's different in the daytime. Alien.

We are in Studio A, running one of the *pas de deuxs* while Morgan offers his opinion on how Sebastian could hold me differently in the lift for better lines. Sebastian agrees with this and tries again.

A few steps are changed, and we both like the tweaks to the choreography.

Other dancers are at the far end of the room practicing other parts, but I can feel their eyes on me. Do they notice the strange tension with me, Sebastian, and Morgan? Can they tell Sebastian and Morgan are related?

Both men keep a professional distance in rehearsal, neither of them touching me too long or with too much familiarity. But after lunch, Morgan pulls me into an alcove in the hallway, kissing and pawing at me. One of the dancers in the corps catches us, but Morgan doesn't pull away. The man has not an ounce of shame. I bury my head in his chest, wanting to disappear.

Great. Everyone in the company will hear about this. They think I'm dating Sebastian. They won't accept them both. In their minds, I'll be a cheater. A whore. The deeper truth that I'm the captive firebird of both men would be too far out of their experience to comprehend or accept. And maybe that's for the best because if my blackmailers go down, I go down with them.

I'm exhausted by the time I get home—physically and mentally. I just want to lie down and catch up on so much of the sleep I've lost over the past few nights. But when I go to my room, the sheets are stripped off my bed. All my personal belongings are gone.

I run to the closet to find nothing but empty hangers. There's a crisp white envelope on the bed. I pull out the paper and unfold it to read the note in what I assume is either Sebastian or Morgan's handwriting.

My dearest firebird, your things have been moved to your newly appointed cage. Sleep on the bare mattress if you must, but Wednesday you are ours. Nine p.m. And this time, we won't be letting you go at midnight. You'll find your key on the kitchen counter.

Below the note is the address to their penthouse. There's a challenge in these words. They want me to choose to come to them now—early. I don't know exactly how Sebastian got into my house. Maybe he took my key from my bag one night when I was blindfolded and gave it to Morgan to make a copy. It's the only possibility I can think of.

I should have activated the alarm, but I rarely bother during the day. I didn't think there was a need. I go to Conall's home office and pull up the security footage from earlier in the day. I watch video of the moving van pull up. Movers emerge with boxes and disappear inside the house which is pretty much what I expected to see. After all, Morgan and Sebastian were with me all day.

I sleep on the bare mattress, unwilling to run to them just because they took my things away.

During rehearsal on Tuesday, Sebastian whispers in my ear, "You *will* be at the penthouse on Wednesday."

"Or you'll report me?" I hiss under my breath.

"Yes." He practically growls the word. I don't know if I believe him. But I'm also not sure I don't. The crazed possessive look in his eyes tells me he'll do whatever it takes to gain my compliance. And if they lose me, I lose everything.

On Wednesday, I use the last of the warm vanilla bath oil to take a bath. The movers didn't take it when they were packing. I guess they were told just to focus on my bedroom.

I sprinkle in rose petals, light candles, and perversely listen to the Firebird music as I lean back against the tub, the steam rising off my skin. Somehow it was so much easier when everything was a mystery behind a blindfold. The truth is too big for me. The reality of the power imbalance remains the same, but before, shielded in the darkness of the blindfold, it was like an erotic dream. Now it feels so much more real. I don't know if I can do this.

Maybe they wouldn't report me to the police. Maybe they aren't *that* cruel. But they could put me back in the corps.

These men have that kind of power. I don't want to believe they'd use their money in the same way Conall used it, to clip my wings. But if these were good men, they wouldn't have done the things they've done to me already.

Finally, I get out of the tub. I wash my hair in the shower. The only clothes I have left are a plum-colored leotard and tights the movers missed because they were in the dryer. I'm angry they've taken all my choices away, that my illusion of freedom is disappearing. But this house is so big and lonely, and there are so many bad memories. Is moving out of it the worst thing in the world?

I get ready exactly as I've gotten ready every Wednesday night, and put the jeans and T-shirt I was wearing back on over my dancewear. Then I take the key off the counter, get in my car, and drive to my new cage.

IT'S A FEW MINUTES PAST NINE WHEN I WALK INTO THE LARGE lobby of the high-rise building.

A security guard nods in greeting when he sees me. "Good evening, Ms. Lane. They're expecting you."

"H-hello," I say, startled that he was given my name.

His gaze goes to my throat, and I swear he knows that it's not just some pretty piece of jewelry. From the lust in his eyes, he knows. And he said *they're* waiting for me. I swallow past the lump in my throat and hurry past him.

Inside the elevator, I use my key to unlock access to the penthouse floor. I take slow shuddering breaths as the elevator lurches upward to my doom. I fantasize about it reaching the top, then going into a free fall so I don't have to face these men again.

I'm not sure these few days of *space* have done anything to soothe my nerves or help me accept this new reality. It feels like the opposite. It's only given me space to run through the mazes in my mind, freaking myself out more and more about everything. Part of me wishes they'd simply demanded my obedience, that Morgan hadn't been soft with me, or that Sebastian had refused the suggestion to give me space.

When I open the door to the penthouse, I walk in to an empty room. "Hello?"

Sebastian and Morgan appear suddenly from opposite doors on either side of me, like wolves circling prey.

"Hello, little rabbit," Morgan says, reinforcing this impression.

I drop my bag on the floor and my keys on the counter. My hands are shaking. My gaze drifts to the giant windows. A ballet barre has been set up there.

"Go to the barre," Sebastian says.

But I don't go to the barre. Instead, I pace back and forth like a caged animal. The tears come then. "Please... I can't." I glance up to find Sebastian raising an eyebrow at this pronouncement.

"You can't go to the barre? That's an odd issue for a ballerina."

"I can't do this!" I shout.

"Morgan, get the cane."

Morgan pushes off the wall to follow this instruction.

For the second time in this penthouse, I crumple to my knees. I can't think of anything else to do but beg for mercy that isn't coming.

"What the fuck is wrong with you?" Sebastian says. "We've been doing this shit for months, and you've seemed happy enough to obey."

"It's different now." I can't explain it, but the spell is broken. The shift away from the opera house, the loss of mystery, the loss of the safety of the blindfold and the certainty that I must obey, that I can't negotiate, that it's safe to accept the pleasure because I have no choice. Now it feels like I have choices, even though I don't think I really do. I'm not sure anymore.

How can I make this choice without the blindfold and the secrets? How can I choose not just one man, but two? It feels so wrong to give myself to two men. It feels as though the secret they kept from me has broken some sacred bond that I thought was just me and Sebastian.

"Fucking Frederick," Morgan says. He's returned with the cane. He passes it to Sebastian, and I tense.

If Frederick hadn't gotten hurt backstage, Sebastian's hand wouldn't have been forced. He wouldn't have had to choose to save both me and his ballet by joining me on stage. If I'd had any thought that he might have orchestrated that reveal, that he wanted me to see him, I was wrong.

"You didn't plan to ever let me see you, or to know about Morgan, did you?" I ask.

"No," Sebastian says. "You were never going to see us, but I was working toward introducing you to the idea that there were two of us."

I'm sobbing now. "I want it back. I don't know how to get it back. I can't let myself..." I don't know how to say these things inside me. They aren't the only ones angry with Frederick. I'm angry, too.

Everything was perfect.

I jump when the cane clatters on the floor, and then Sebastian is beside me. He pulls me into his arms. He frees my hair from the bun and smooths his fingers through it. "Shhh, you're safe."

I only cry harder. I wanted him to say those words last week... so badly. I know they're true—at least to an extent. These past few days in my own house have at least given me that perspective.

"We won't report you to the police as long as you don't report us," Sebastian says. "We wouldn't harm you like that. But you belong to us. You know that, right, Cassia? We won't let you go."

Morgan sits on the ground on the other side of me and starts stroking my back. "Just give in to us," he says.

"You said you'd report me. You said it *recently!*" I say to Sebastian, trying to ignore Morgan's soothing touch. The million ways I've been betrayed by this man... by both of them... I can't...

Sebastian sighs. "I know what I said. Everything felt out of control."

Yes. That's it. Everything is out of control. *How do I get it back?*

"Undress," Sebastian says. He and Morgan help me stand.

I hesitate. I want to do this. I want things to go back, but I don't know how to make this choice. I don't know how to let myself do this. Then Morgan is behind me, tying the blindfold around my eyes.

"Undress," Sebastian says again. He's moved a few feet away from me. I hear the distance in his voice.

Suddenly, I'm back in the opera house. Everything is normal again. Cello music begins to play out of the sound system, and I take off my outer layer of clothes. I stand there, now in leotard and tights, hesitating.

"Undress. It's the final time I'm telling you. You're already getting a punishment for your resistance."

I peel the leotard and tights off.

"Good girl," Sebastian says. "Now kneel for your punishment. You know how I like you."

And now it's back, that throbbing and wetness between my legs. Just like that. So simple. I'm helped into a kneeling position on a soft rug, so I don't have to kneel on the hard floor.

My arms stretch out before me, my palms on the hardwood. My forehead rests there as well.

"Please, Master... not the cane."

"Yes, the cane," he practically growls. "You need to remember who you belong to, and nothing drives it home like the cane."

I'm crying again. But part of it is relief. Because I've given in. I've surrendered. I will do whatever he says. I will do whatever Morgan says. They will punish me, and then they will fuck me, and we will have breached this final boundary between us. And it will all be perfect again.

"You will count," Sebastian says. "I will give you five, and then Morgan will give you five. Say, yes, Master."

"Y-yes, Master," I whisper. I want to beg him because ten is too many. I can't take ten. But I need things back in control. I need to return to the peaceful calm place inside my head that Sebastian gives me.

"Say it so the cheap seats can hear it," Sebastian says.

Morgan chuckles at this.

"Yes, Master," I say louder.

"Good girl."

Everything inside me relaxes at these words.

The cane slices through the air, and I flinch as it strikes my bared ass. But it isn't as hard as the last time he did it, the time when I made thirty-two mistakes. It hurts, it sears and burns into my flesh, but I know he's holding back just enough that I can take it.

"One," I say. I take long, slow breaths and fall into a rhythm with him. My surrender, his power. This exquisite torment.

After the fifth one, he passes the cane to Morgan.

The sixth strike makes me scream. I thought Morgan was the soft one. The kind one. I'm immediately disabused of this notion.

"Master, please!" I shriek.

Morgan laughs. "It's about time you said my name. Count," he demands.

"S-six," I whimper.

"Good girl."

It's the first time I've heard these words from Morgan, and they're just as satisfying from his mouth as from Sebastian's.

Seven and Eight are just as hard as Six. I scream with each strike. I worry other people living in this high rise are going to think they're killing me. Wouldn't it be fucked up if some random person called the police on all of us?

Suddenly a hand is gripping my chin, turning my tear-streaked face upward.

"Do I need to gag you?" Morgan asks.

"N-no, Master. Please..."

He pulls back a little on Nine. A welcome relief. But the final lash is just as hard as his first. I bite back the scream and count the last one. I'm so shockingly wet right now.

I feel the cane press against the top of my head. "Lift your head up and kiss it," Morgan says.

I rise up and kiss the bamboo.

"Now thank me for your punishment."

"Thank you, Master."

One of them, I don't know which, dips a finger between my legs and inside my pussy.

"Are you ready to be fucked?" Sebastian asks.

"Y-yes, Master."

"By both of us? Are you ready to take both of us, together?"

My face flames, but I say, "Yes, Master."

"Good girl."

The finger is withdrawn, and one of them helps me to stand. He leads me to the bedroom. I hear zippers and clothes hitting the floor.

"Straddle and ride me," Sebastian orders.

He's lying on the bed. My knees are on either side of him. I let out a gasp of pleasure as I lower myself onto his thick, hardened cock. I forgot he was this big. He gives me time to adjust.

"Fuck," he says. But it isn't an expression of pleasure. It's a command.

I obey, raising and lowering myself on him. I've forgotten for a moment about Morgan, until I feel him licking the cane welts on my ass.

"Poor little rabbit," he says. He rubs a soothing balm over the marks as I continue to ride Sebastian.

A few moments later, I feel cold lubed metal being worked inside my ass. "Open for me," Morgan orders. "It's going to be my dick in a minute."

I try to relax as he pushes the toy inside me. The double-penetration of the toy in my ass and Sebastian in my pussy is overwhelming in a way that erases all logical thought. Every doubt and fear fades away in this moment. Every protest of what I can and cannot do evaporates in the sheer visceral power of this moment.

Morgan removes the toy, and then it's his lubed cock sliding inside my ass. I tense at first because he's so much bigger, and I'm afraid, but he strokes my back and eases in more slowly. Once he gets past the tight band of muscle, he gives me a moment. Both men still, letting me adjust to this fullness, this sense of being completely overtaken by them.

"Are you okay, cupcake?" Sebastian asks, stroking my face.

"Yes, Master."

He rips the blindfold off, and I'm staring now into his dark, intense eyes, that vicious scar. I reach out and stroke the scar. This time, he doesn't stop me. Then the three of us begin to move together in an intoxicating hypnotic rhythm. I come first, moaning and screaming out my orgasm, not caring that neighbors might hear us.

Sebastian and Morgan come together after me.

"Fuck yes," Morgan growls behind me.

Morgan pulls out of me first and lifts me off Sebastian. Then we are a tangle of limbs. I lay in the middle. I'm facing Morgan now. He strokes my face, while Sebastian runs his fingertips gently over my cane marks.

Morgan leans forward and kisses me on the mouth, his tongue tangling with mine. Sebastian twists my body, opening my legs wide, and then his mouth is between my legs, his tongue moving inside me. I whimper and writhe, my moans being swallowed up by Morgan's mouth.

Sebastian is relentless, licking and sucking me until another orgasm comes crashing over me. When it's over, I think they'll let me rest, but they only change places. Sebastian moves up to my mouth, letting me taste myself on his tongue, while Morgan's mouth is between my legs drawing out the same agonizing pleasure from my body.

Then they are both ready to fuck me again. This goes on most of the night. I lose track of time of reality and of all the reasons why I was so sure I couldn't do this. It all melts into my moans of pleasure.

Finally, I beg them to stop. I need to rest. I need sleep. Reluctantly, they pull out of me. We sleep together, the three of us in the large bed. And it feels like something very important has shifted. They're right, I belong to them. They won't let me go, but this time I don't want to fly away.

EPILOGUE

It's opening night of a new season. I stand in the wings before the curtain rises, waiting to go onstage. Sebastian leans close to my ear. "Don't disappoint me, firebird."

I laugh. "I'm really scared if you don't know which ballet we're doing."

"Just keeping you on your toes. And the sass ends as soon as we get home. Understand?"

"Y-Yes, Master," I whisper so the other nearby dancers don't hear. I don't know how he still keeps me on this knife edge of fear and desire. Even as I know who he is. Even as I know I can trust him. I've finally come to accept my life is safe in his hands—in both men's hands.

He leans in again and whispers. "You'll always be my firebird."

A low jolt of desire runs through me as the curtain rises.

We dance Prokofiev's Romeo and Juliet. Each time his hands are on me in a *pas de deux*, it feels like a tease. His hands are on me, but they aren't on me in the way I need for them to be on me. Henry was right that it's as if we are fucking on stage. The audience can feel it, too.

In some perverse way, they're watching burlesque right now, not ballet. But they love it. They drink it up like desperate parched people lost in a desert. Everyone in the audience knows that this man owns me, body and soul. Even if they don't know they know it. Even the dimmest among them cannot possibly miss the erotically possessive way his hands move on me as we dance. Even the most innocent touch telegraphs sex.

They're transfixed by our interpretation of the star-crossed lovers. We take our final bows; the applause of the crowd is thunderous. The audience surges to their feet. Bouquets of fresh flowers are tossed at ours. We are *perfection*.

I wonder if our sophisticated moneyed voyeurs will have the same passion we share tonight. I wonder if our energy somehow fed something inside them... a visual aphrodisiac. The roars of the crowd continue forever, and we stand there drinking it all in, letting their energy charge us.

A large bouquet of dark red roses is tossed from the private box where Morgan watched us dance. I tentatively step forward and take the bouquet from the stage. There's a card. I pull it out and read.

Be ready, little rabbit. The wolves are hungry tonight.

Sebastian squeezes my hand. My gaze goes to his, and he holds me there, trapped and pinned by the knowledge of what he will demand of my body soon. What they both will demand. They're predators, and I am their prey. And when this curtain goes down, the chase will begin.

※

I HOPE YOU ENJOYED PERFECTION. IF YOU'RE NEW TO MY work, please accept this free novella, THREE WORDS, available exclusively for download from my website: https://kittythomas.com/free-book/

I'D ALSO LIKE TO INVITE YOU TO CHECK OUT MY COMPLETED Pleasure House series, starting with GUILTY PLEASURES (available on sale for 99 cents!)

OTHER BUY LINKS HERE: HTTPS://KITTYTHOMAS.COM/BOOK/ guilty-pleasures/

GUILTY PLEASURES:

SHE WAS A BORED HOUSEWIFE UNTIL SHE WAS TAKEN AND TRAINED for the pleasure of the highest bidder.

VIVIAN DELANEY LEADS A LIFE OF PRIVILEGE, BUT BEHIND CLOSED doors she feels isolated and trapped in a gilded cage. Unable to achieve sexual pleasure with her husband, she finds herself in the capable hands of Anton, a massage therapist intent on awakening her to her full sexual potential. By any means necessary.

FOR A LIST OF ALL MY TITLES, PLEASE GO HERE: HTTPS://kittythomas.com/reading-order-for-new-readers/

. . .

I LOVE HEARING FROM MY READERS, FEEL FREE TO CONTACT ME at: https://kittythomas.com/contact

THANK YOU FOR READING!

KITTY ^.^